The Little Swans Fly East

The Little Swans Fly East

Carolyn Swift

With illustrations by Carol Betera

POOLBEG

Published 1995 by
Poolbeg Press Ltd,
Knocksedan House,
123 Baldoyle Industrial Estate,
Dublin 13, Ireland

A catalogue record for this book is available from the British Library.

ISBN 1 85371 449 6

Illustrations by Carol Betera
Cover design by Poolbeg Group Services Ltd
Set by Poolbeg Group Services Ltd in Garamond 11/14
Printed by The Guernsey Press Ltd,
Vale, Guernsey, Channel Islands.

To all the parents and teachers with whom I travelled to Perm over Easter, 1994, and all the students and staff of the State Choreographic Institute, who made our visit such a fascinating and enjoyable one.

Contents

The Little Swans Fly East

As the long train pulled out of Moscow's Yaroslavskiy Station, whoops and cheers echoed down the corridor from the boys' carriage. Gráinne and Sinéad cheered too, but Bernie stood in silence in the open carriage doorway, staring out of the corridor window, too excited even to speak. At last they were really on their way to the State Choreographic Institute.

It was hard to believe it was only thirteen months since she had first dared to dream of training in Russia. Her hopes had grown from the moment Madame Chumakova had spoken at the end of her first ballet summer school in Dublin, even though Bernie hadn't been able to finish the classes because of a back injury. As she had sat with the small audience of parents and teachers, applauding the other students in the "Dance of the Little Swans" from *Swan Lake*, which they had all learned during the fortnight, the little Russian woman with the sloe-black eyes and ramrod-straight back had made the announcement.

"In the Spring," she had said, "I come back to Ireland to find students for my school in Russia and there is chance for some of you."

She had added, as she always did, "If you work

1

hard!" and Bernie had never worked harder. From that moment she had thought and dreamed of nothing else. Every penny she could earn by doing odd jobs, or could coax from her father's earnings as a bus-driver or her mother's takings from her Moore Street fruit and vegetable stall, was spent on extra classes to add to her regular ones at the MARIE BYRNE SCHOOL OF DANCE. And when she wasn't at class or at school or earning extra cash from odd jobs, she was down at the public library in the Ilac Centre, trying to learn Russian from their Linguaphone course.

As the train slowly ambled past a large, imposing-looking building, she tried to read the words painted over the doorway, but they might as well have been in Arabic. Learning phrases on cassette was no help in making sense of this strange Russian writing full of backward capital Rs and upsidedown small hs. Then shrieks of laughter from behind her made her turn to face the others again. Inside the narrow, overheated carriage, Sinéad's tiny figure was completely enveloped in the folds of a cotton blanket, which Amanda had pulled down from the top bunk.

"Sorry!" Amanda giggled, helping Gráinne to disentangle her cousin from its off-white folds, "but Bernie's bedding seems to be up there as well as mine."

Bernie looked at Amanda's flowered dressing-gown and spongebag, lying on the top bunk as proof of ownership.

"And who says the top bunk's yours?" she demanded.

"I bagsed it," Amanda told her. "It's your own fault if you were too busy gazing out the window."

Bernie glanced across at the top bunk on the other

side of the carriage, but Gráinne's woolly hat and gloves lay on that.

"It's not fair," she complained. "If yous all want top bunks we oughta toss for them."

"I don't mind the bottom bunk," Sinéad said.

"Well, bully for you," snapped Amanda, "but I want to see out. The bottom of the window's all steamed up."

"Can't you give it a bit of a rub?" Bernie argued impatiently, wiping at the window with the sleeve of her gabardine, but it remained obstinately misty.

"I already tried that," Amanda pointed out, "but there's two lots of glass and the steam's in the middle. Anyway, I want the top bunk."

"And you always get what you want, of course," Bernie retorted, "only you see things are different now. You're not in your Mammy's school any more. In Russia we'll all be equal."

"Oh no, we won't," Amanda argued. "We'll be graded according to talent and experience."

"Oh, for Heaven's sake!" Gráinne exploded, "don't be such babies! Can't Bernie have the top bunk on this side if it's so important. It's getting dark now anyway and soon there'll be nothing to see."

"And if we're both on bottom bunks it'll be easier to talk when we're in bed," Sinéad told her.

"Thanks, Gráinne," Bernie said. "I always feel like I'm suffocating in a bottom bunk, ever since I had one in the youth hostel."

"Let's get them made up now while the train's still crawling," Gráinne suggested. "They'll be much harder to do when it starts lurching about."

The train certainly seemed in no hurry, Bernie

thought. No wonder the journey took twenty-two hours. She looked around for some sort of stepladder to sort out the two piles of bedding on the top bunk but there was no sign of one.

"I guess you just stand on the lower bunk and haul yourself up," Gráinne said, as if she could read Bernie's thoughts. "There doesn't seem to be any sort of let-down ladder."

"Easy for the likes of us," Bernie told her, as she swung herself up lightly, "but you'd wonder how those fat old wrinklies that were doing all that pushing and shoving on the platform are gonna manage. Maybe they're all fighting now over the bottom bunks."

"Pity you're not sharing with them so," Amanda said nastily, but Bernie ignored her. There would be plenty of time to show Amanda she was no longer top dog.

As they crouched in the narrow space between the carriage ceiling and the top bunk, dividing up the little pile of towels and blankets, she thought again how unfair it had been that Miss Byrne could give her daughter extra coaching. She had made sure that whoever failed Madame Chumakova's audition last Easter, it wouldn't be Amanda.

Bernie had thought about this the night before the audition, tossing and turning in the bed she shared with her younger sister, Kylie. Her whole future hung on one little class. And if she were not picked to go to Russia, she felt she would die. But then, even if she were picked, would her father ever let her go?

"Do yous both think I'm made of money?" he had demanded, when Bernie's mother had backed her pleas to be allowed to go. "An' if I was to win the Lotto itself I hope I'd have more sense than let you go. You'd have to be astray in the head to think of ruinin' your chance of a bit of education to go gallivantin' off to bloody Russia, if yous don't mind!"

"But I'd be learning Russian," Bernie had pleaded, "an' French an' the piano, as well as the dancing."

"I dunno what class of a job yous think they'd give you above in Gateaux with qualifications the like of that!" her father had jeered.

"Ah, Da!" Bernie had wailed. "Don't ya know they're not taking on any more in Gateaux and from all I hear they're likely to be layin' people off. An' anyways, I don't want a job in Gateaux. I wanta be a dancer!"

"Ah, for the love an' honour!" her father had groaned, "will ya switch over and try the other side! That song's long past its sell-by date."

But Bernie had kept on begging and pleading until finally she had worn her father down.

"Will ya ever give over before ya have us all drove outa house an' home!" he had shouted in the end. "If ya get the bloomin' audition I'll think about it."

"Fantastic!" Bernie had cried, flinging her arms around his neck.

"That'll do ya now," he had mumbled. "I only said I'd *think* about it. It's a quare old sum for people the like of us to have to come up with."

"How many d'ya think she'll take?" Bernie had asked her friend Eileen, walking home from class the following day.

"Miss Byrne said eleven or twelve," Eileen told her, "but if it was only half that she'd take you, I'm sure she would. Didn't you tell me she always called you 'her little swan'? She must like you."

"She called us all her little swans when she was teaching us the dance," Bernie said. "And anyways liking doesn't come into it. It's how I dance at the audition that's gonna count and I'm scared stiff I'm going to blow it. Are you going for it?"

"What's the use," Eileen shrugged, "an' me gettin' turned down for the Summer School? An' anyways Mammy says she doesn't know how she's gonna raise the money for one, don't mind two."

"Larry's going for it then?" Bernie asked.

"Don't you know he is!" Eileen said in disgust, "an' him only a wet day learning. But Willie Moran has his mind made up they'll be going together."

"Maybe they will so," Bernie agreed reluctantly. "Madame wants boys for her school an' there's not likely to be that many up for it."

"Only them two and Michael Smythe," Eileen suggested and Bernie hadn't been surprised on the day of the audition to find that Eileen's younger brother and the other two boys from Miss Byrne's were, indeed, the only ones there.

By contrast there were twenty girls along with herself, though that was better odds than she had dared to hope. It had seemed more than likely that all twenty-nine from the Summer School would be there and maybe more besides.

"Why isn't Janet here?" she whispered to Michael Smythe, beside her at the *barre*. "I thought she'd walk it."

"Her parents wouldn't let her come," Michael told her. "She has her Leaving to do and so has Mary. I'm only surprised to see Barbara and Joan here. They must be coming up to their Leaving too."

"So are you," Bernie retorted, for Michael was the oldest in her class.

"Ah, but my parents always knew I'd have a career in theatre," Michael said grandly. "My Dad never bothered with the Leaving and look at him now!"

Bernie had sighed, wishing for the umpteenth time that her father too was a film star.

"Would you ever let me finish making up my bed first, before you do yours?" Gráinne cried in exasperation, after Sinéad had bumped into her for the third time. "There's just not room for both of us to work away at the same time."

"OK," Sinéad agreed. "I'll wait outside till you're finished. It's cooler out there."

In the corridor she found a small tip-up seat, but she was too short to see much through the window from a sitting position and soon she was on her feet again, staring out at the endless forests of birch trees and scotch pine in the fading light.

"Oo, look at the funny little houses!" she shouted, as the train passed a huddle of small dachaus in a forest clearing, but there was no reply. Probably they couldn't hear her inside in the carriage, although she had left the sliding door half-open.

The youngest in the group, Sinéad could still hardly believe she had been accepted for Madame Chumakova's school. Unlike Bernie, Gráinne and Amanda, she hadn't even been in the top class at that first summer school. She remembered how upset she had been when Larry had been moved up from her class into the top one, although he too was only a beginner. But that was when Madame Chumakova had first raised her hopes.

"Boy's body different from girl's body," she had explained. "Boys do not dance *sur les pointes*. You try too much too soon you do damage, spoil everything. But you good girl. Work hard and maybe one day you become professional dancer."

Sinéad had not even known if she would be allowed to go to Russia. A former Irish dance champion, her mother had always disapproved of ballet and it was only because Madame Chumakova had persuaded her that she had let Sinéad take classes at all. But her cousin Gráinne had come up from Cork to stay with them in order to go to the audition and Sinéad had gone along with her, just as she had done to see the students from Madame's school dance at the National Concert Hall the previous June.

Reminding herself that she was two years younger than Gráinne, who had – after all – been training at the O'Connell School in Cork since she was ten, Sinéad hadn't expected to be accepted this time. She could have another try next year, she told herself and, failing that, the year after. Meantime Gráinne, who would be sure to be accepted, could tell her all about the school so she would have a head start when she did go.

In this frame of mind she was not really nervous at the audition, which was much like the first day of the summer school, when Madame was trying to decide in which class to place them. Anxious to show Madame Chumakova how hard she had been working, she simply did her best, conscious always of those black piercing eyes darting here and there, studying the feet, the legs, the back, the shoulders, the arms, the hands and the head. At the end of class, when Madame said, "Thank you!" and they made their *reverences*, she had told them nothing, merely smiling at Bernie and asking, "No more trouble with back?"

"On no, Madame," Bernie had assured her feverishly, and Sinéad had felt a tinge of jealousy that Madame had remembered Bernie and would surely pick her. But then Bernie's exit from the summer school had been so dramatic it was hardly surprising she would be remembered.

"And I've loads of time," she reminded herself.

So it was that she was taken totally by surprise when the letter came.

"*A Mhaimí, a Mhaimí!*" she had cried, charging into her mother's room. "I've been offered a place at Madame Chumakova's school in Russia. Please may I go? Oh, please! *Más é do thoil é, a Mhaimí!*"

She had waited in a fever of anxiety, but whatever Madame Chumakova had said to her mother at the summer school must have had a remarkable effect. Instead of the indignant denunciation of ballet as a foreign dance, which Sinéad had half-expected, her mother was full of congratulations.

"*Maith an cailín!*" she cried. "And you only a beginner! Isn't that living proof of what a good grounding in Irish dance will do for you? But you're very young to be going off to Russia. I didn't think she'd take anyone still under fourteen."

"But I'm well able to mind myself, Mam, honest!"

Sinéad protested. "And they start learning ballet in Russia when they're only eight."

"Maybe so, but it's a long way from home at your age," her mother said.

"But I won't be by myself," Sinéad pleaded. "There'll be ten or eleven others going from here and Gráinne's sure to be one of them."

"I'd certainly feel easier in my mind if Gráinne was there to keep an eye on you," her mother agreed, "but it's a big decision to take. Your father and I will have to talk it over. In the meantime let's ring your Aunt Nan and found out if Gráinne really is going."

That had been the start of months of frenzied planning until September arrived in a sudden rush, after months when Sinéad had felt it would never come. As if in a dream she had found herself with Gráinne amongst the small group of excited boys and girls gathered around their escort at Dublin Airport.

"Whatever can you see in all that darkness?"

Sinéad jumped at the sound of Willie's voice. Her thoughts had been so far away she hadn't heard him coming down the corridor towards her.

"Nothing much," she said. "Lights from houses now and then."

"Doesn't sound very exciting," Willie laughed. "You were so still I thought maybe you could see eyes like torch beams in the forest: foxes maybe, or even wolves."

"They'd want to be pretty dumb to show themselves when they can hear the train a mile off," Sinéad shrugged, turning from the window to see Gráinne waving at her from inside the carriage. "I was only thinking. Now I've to make up my bunk."

"I'm not doing mine till bedtime," Willie told her. "I couldn't even if I wanted to. Everyone's sitting on it."

He watched Sinéad struggle with the coarse blanket until Amanda gave him a dirty look and slid the carriage door shut with a bang. He had hoped they could have a bit of a laugh for, although he and Larry had been having great crack in their carriage, Richard had more or less frozen him out of it.

Returning to the school for a second year, Richard was even older than Michael, but the two of them were already deep in quiet conversation and complaining to Larry and Willie about the noise. They had met Richard when they had all been allowed to do class with him and the Russian boys in June before the Ballet Gala in the National Concert Hall and Michael and Richard had become friends at once.

Doing class with the Russians had really opened Willie's eyes. He had thought Michael good in the simple Russian dance he had done in the Rupert Guinness Hall at the end of Willie's first term at Miss Byrne's, but when he saw the Russian boys dance a *gopak* he was struck dumb. They could jump so high! Even standing behind them at the *barre* was electrifying. They could raise their legs to a remarkable angle! He had always been teased at Miss Byrne's for having the nerve to try anything, but even he was a little shaken now at the thought of what he was taking on.

"The lads going out to the Olympics have nothing on this bunch!" Larry had muttered in his ear in the dressing-room after their first class and Willie had had to hide a smile. Larry, after all, was the athlete and gymnast who had for so long refused to learn dancing because he thought it was sissy. He obviously thought differently now.

Suddenly the corridor was flooded with light as the train swung alongside city streets and into a station, shuddering to a stop. Willie could hear doors opening all down the train and saw people collecting in little groups on the platform. He thought it must be a large city that so many were getting out until he noticed less than half of them were crossing the line by the sleepers towards the exit on the far side. The others, without baggage, seemed to be swelling the little groups he had already noticed.

"What's going on?" asked a voice and Willie saw Larry had joined him.

"I dunno," Willie said, "and you can't open these windows to stick your head out. Let's go down to the door."

Larry followed him down the corridor past the hot water urn that Richard called the samovar to the door. When Willie opened it a welcome blast of cool air hit them as they stood, high above the platform, peering out.

"They're buying something," Willie exclaimed. "Let's go and see what it is. We must be stopping here for ages if all those ould ones are getting out. I don't know how some of them managed it. It's quite a jump down."

Just then a Russian came from the further compartment and, muttering something they couldn't understand, shouldered them aside. He opened a little hatch beside the door and three iron steps tumbled down, like a mini fire escape, though it still didn't quite reach the platform.

"Come on!" Willie cried and he and Larry hurried down the steps after him.

As they ran down the platform they passed a woman with a child who was eating ice cream.

"They're selling ices!" Larry cried. "I wonder how much they are?"

But when they reached the first group they found only an old woman selling packets of rather dull-looking biscuits, arranged on a tray hung from her shoulders.

"Further on!" Larry shouted, as the two boys raced on to the next group.

This seemed to melt away just as they reached it, leaving only three old women, one of whom had a long red sausage under her arm.

"Where are they getting the ices?" Larry asked, but the other groups all seemed to have disappeared.

The woman held out the sausage and Willie suddenly felt hungry. The hostel they had stayed in overnight in Moscow had once been the home of a famous Russian composer. It had been palatial-looking from outside, set in its own formal gardens like a stately home you would pay to see over on a Sunday at home in Ireland, but breakfast had been a sort of lumpy porridge made from something called *kasha* and the lunch had been thin, fatty soup with a few small chicken bones swimming around in it, followed by cucumber salad. The sausage had to be an improvement on that.

Willie fished in his pockets and brought out a few notes but, before he could even attempt to ask how

Looking up, he saw to his horror that
the train was moving.

much the sausage was, the woman pounced on one of them and thrust the sausage into his arms, shouting something he didn't understand and waving towards the train. Then he became aware of more shouting. Looking up, he saw to his horror that the train was moving.

Opening Positions

With the long red sausage held in one hand like the baton in a relay race, Willie started to run.

"This way!" Larry yelled and Willie saw he was sprinting like the Community Games champion runner he was towards the front of the train.

By the time the two boys reached the platform's edge, the engine was already out of sight around a bend in the track and the seventh and eighth carriages were slowly lumbering past, with all their steps hauled in and their firmly-closed doors at shoulder height. Then Willie became aware of shouts from an open door in the tenth carriage, where a man stood on top of the three iron steps, waving his arms.

As he drew level with them the two boys leaped for the steps, nearly pulling the man from the train as he tried to haul them in. For a second the three of them swayed precariously on the steps, clinging to the door, the door frame and one another. Finally they fell inwards on to the moving plates between the tenth and eleventh carriages, leaving the door swinging dangerously behind them. As he disentangled himself from the boys and picked himself up, the man muttered something in Russian which Willie, still firmly clutching his sausage, felt it was just as well he couldn't understand. Then he found his English.

"You crazy boys! Never you leave the train without I say!" he shouted angrily and, as he pressed the lever to fold back the steps and struggled to close the swinging door, Willie saw that it was Yuri.

Yuri was the tall, fair-haired Russian who had met them at Moscow airport and taken them to the waiting coach. He had explained that he would be in charge of them until they reached the school and that next morning he would take them on a quick coach tour of Moscow before travelling with them on the overnight Kama Express. He was sharing a compartment with three Russian men, but had first found them their compartments, made sure they each had blankets, sheets and towels, told them where the toilets were and that they could get hot water for their tea bags and jars of instant coffee from the samovar at the end of the carriage.

"I'm sorry, Yuri," Willie stammered, "but everyone else got out."

"They know how long train stop," Yuri snapped.

"How?" asked Larry.

"Is written here," Yuri told him, stabbing with his finger at a framed notice on the wall between two windows.

Willie looked at it, but it was in strange lettering.

"I can't make head or tail of it," he said, "though I guess MOCKBA is Moscow because it's the first place on the list."

"So always you ask me before you leave train," Yuri said. "Now please, go to your compartment. Already you make problem enough for one day."

Walking up the lurching train like drunken sailors past carriage after carriage full of dozing Russians, although it was only eight o'clock even by Russian time, Willie and Larry bumped into Gráinne and Sinéad, who were filling two mugs each with boiling water from the samovar.

"You'd want to look where you're going with a dangerous weapon like that!" Gráinne giggled, at the sight of the long red sausage sticking out from under Willie's arm. "Wherever did you get it?"

"Bought it at the last stop," Willie said casually, glad that the girls had apparently missed their undignified scramble back on to the train. "D'you want some of it?"

"I wouldn't mind trying a piece if you can spare it," Gráinne said. "The sandwiches they gave us aren't very exciting."

"We ate our sambos ages ago," Larry told her. "I was starved with the hunger."

"We'd better take Amanda and Bernie the hot water for their tea bags," Sinéad said. "Can we come back for a piece of sausage?"

"I'll have to get the penknife out of my rucksack first anyways," Larry told her.

"So why don't you get your mugs at the same time and join us?" Gráinne said. "We could make it a party."

"Then they'd have to give some sausage to Bernie and Amanda too," Sinéad pointed out.

"That's OK," Willie said. "I'd sooner share it with them than Michael and Richard."

The sausage was very fatty and Amanda refused her share.

"All the more for us!" Willie crowed, as she wrinkled up her nose at his offering.

And, eaten between the slices of unbuttered bread which sandwiched their thin pieces of processed cheese, Bernie thought it made the best meal they had had all day, especially with the cheese left in. So, sitting side by side on Gráinne and Sinéad's bunks, laughing, chattering and swilling cups of tea, the time passed quickly until Yuri hammered on the compartment door and told them the Russians next door were complaining they were being kept awake. But even after Larry and Willie had returned to their own compartments and the four girls had climbed into their bunks, Bernie lay awake for what seemed like a long time.

What would it really be like, this school she had dreamed about for so long? Madame Chumakova was a wonderful teacher and had always been kind to her, as well as speaking good English, but she only taught the graduate class. Suppose Bernie was in a class with a horrible teacher who could speak nothing but Russian? And suppose the Russian students had no time for Irish girls who hadn't been at a Russian ballet school from the age of eight? And would she ever get the hang of the piano? Unlike Amanda, who had had piano lessons since she was ten, Bernie had never played the piano in her life. It would all be so different from anything she had ever known before.

The compartment lit up as the train pulled into a station and Bernie rolled over on to her elbow and peered out of the window. A few people carrying travel bags or old-fashioned suitcases were moving up the platform beneath her. In the background she could see a lighted building which looked more like a town hall than a station. Otherwise there was nothing to be seen. A notice board under a light probably gave the name of the city but the letters had something like a letter K facing both ways at once and a backward R in it, so Bernie was none the wiser. Puzzling over it she fell asleep and did not stir again until she was wakened by the sound of Gráinne and Sinéad whispering together across the space between the bunks below her.

The sun was shining brightly and she turned on her elbow to look out. There seemed to be little change in the scenery sliding past the window. Was it possible that after twelve hours there was still nothing between cities but birch forest? She obviously wouldn't be passing the rest of the time admiring the view. The primitive wash basin in the toilet, its floor wet from the water only partly disappeared down the drain in the corner after sluicing, hardly encouraged her to spend time in front of its cracked mirror. Nor did she feel like reading in the crowded compartment, now hot and sticky even when the door on to the corridor was left open.

Growing bored with Gráinne and Sinéad's chatter and Amanda's snide remarks, Bernie decided to stretch her legs in the corridor. Turning away from the samovar she lurched in the opposite direction till she reached the compartment occupied by Barbara Jordan, the only other girl from the Marie Byrne School of Dance who was going to the school. She was older than Bernie and from a higher class, but Bernie thought she might be lonely amongst strangers, since her friend Joan, though also offered a place, had finally decided not to interrupt her schooling so close to her Leaving.

When she reached the compartment, however, Barbara seemed already to have bonded with the three girls from dance schools in Limerick, Wexford and Belfast. She asked Bernie if her compartment was equally hot but, after Bernie had said "Worse!" she seemed to have nothing more to say.

On the way back to her own carriage Bernie passed a compartment with four girls who, like Richard, were returning to the school for a second year. Having seen them dancing in the Ballet Gala at the National Concert Hall, Bernie thought of them as superior beings, to be admired and envied rather than talked to. As she passed, however, one of them looked up and gave her a friendly smile. Bernie decided that if she needed help in her strange new surroundings this would be a good person to turn to. Just then Michael came out of the next compartment with Richard and Bernie asked the name of the girl.

"Oh, that's Betty Donnelly," Richard said. "She's a farmer's daughter from somewhere in the Midlands."

He said it as if he thought her someone of no importance, and Bernie was glad she wouldn't be dependent on Richard for directions.

After a while Yuri brought them more sandwiches. This time they were chicken and rather better than the cheese ones of the day before. These were soon eaten, however, and it was not long before they were hoping the train would stop somewhere for long enough to buy something else. But, as if out of spite, the train, which had stopped for a long time before they were up and dressed, never stopped more than a minute or two. Nevertheless, they alarmed Yuri greatly by rushing to the door every time it did stop and opening it wide.

"Train leave again less than one minute!" he cried, hurrying after them. "No one must get out!"

"We're not getting out, Yuri," Amanda told him. "Only getting air!" For the balmy autumn breeze was wonderful after the stifling heat of the compartment.

Yuri looked uneasily at them as they crowded around the open door, not trusting them to stay on the train if he once turned his back on them.

"The Russians don't seem to mind the heat," Gráinne pointed out.

"They seem to sleep the whole time," Sinéad said, for those in the compartment they passed still seemed to be dozing.

"They probably call us the mad Irish," Willie laughed.

"And maybe they're right," Larry told him. "Wouldn't we want to be mad to be breaking our backs to raise the money to stew on this ould train? It never seems to go more than forty miles an hour. D'you think will we ever get there at all?"

But punctually to the minute it arrived. For some time it had been travelling through a heavy industrial area, with black smoke pouring from the top of chimneys in a way that made Gráinne cry out in horror.

"Has nobody here a thought for the environment?" she asked. "I never saw such pollution!"

But before anyone could reply Yuri came down the corridor.

"You get ready now to leave train," he said. "Please have suitcases ready in corridor and forget nothing."

"Is this it?" Bernie asked, looking at the smoking chimneys.

"In two minutes," Yuri told her.

With a strange feeling in her stomach that was half excitement, half fear, Bernie pulled her case from under Sinéad's bunk, put her unread book into the top of it and heaved it out into the corridor.

By now the train had passed the factories and was pulling into a large station with several platforms. When it stopped Bernie followed Yuri from the train and saw him wave to a group a short distance away. Apart from a large, broad-shouldered woman they were all boys. Then Betty and her three companions emerged from the train and suddenly the boys were all around them laughing and chattering in Russian. Listening to Betty and the others talking away in Russian in reply, Bernie understood only a word here and there and wondered if she would ever be able to talk so easily in Russian herself. Then one of the boys turned to her, smiling.

"I take!" he said, holding out his hand for her case.

She felt her arm go slack as he took the weight from her and lifted the case on to a nearby trolley.

"This way!" Yuri called back as he and the large woman strode off down the platform towards a flight of steps.

Bernie and the other newcomers followed as the boys finished loading the rest of the baggage on to the trolley, still laughing and joking with the older girls. Near the foot of the steps a minibus waited and they all clambered in. Bernie had hoped to see something of the place in which she would be spending most of the coming year but, once away from the bright lights of the station, she realised it was growing dark once more. A whole day's sunshine had gone by while they sweated on the so-called "express".

"I take!" he said, holding out his hand for her case.

Ahead of her, Gráinne and Sinéad scrambled into two seats together. Willie and Larry took the two opposite, Barbara and her three friends already had the four seats in front of them and the senior boys and girls had taken over the back of the bus with the luggage, so Bernie had no choice but to sit beside Amanda, opposite Michael and Richard. They all seemed to fall naturally into twos, Bernie thought, and wished for the umpteenth time that Eileen had been with them, for they had always done everything together since they had started at the MARIE BYRNE SCHOOL OF DANCE on the same day. Now she feared she might be paired with Amanda for the whole year and, when they drew up in a tree-lined street between two large buildings and everyone began getting out, she realised with horror she had no one with whom she could share a room.

The large woman led them up the steps of the nearest building, along a passage, up a flight of steep stairs and opened a door on the first floor. The room looked out over the street, but the only thing Bernie noticed was that it had three beds.

"Will we take this if we're let?" she whispered quickly to Gráinne and, when the large woman turned and held up three fingers, was delighted to see Gráinne nod.

"*Spaceboh*," Bernie said gratefully to the woman, as she followed Gráinne and Sinéad into the room.

"*Pozhalsta*," the tall woman smiled back, turning to lead the others to rooms elsewhere.

"I didn't know you could speak Russian!" Sinéad cried in admiration.

"I only know a few words," Bernie said, "but we'd

wanta learn fast. That lady hasn't a word of English, whoever she is."

"I heard Richard telling Michael she was the Administrator," Gráinne told her. "What did you say to her?"

"I only said thanks," Bernie answered.

"And what did she say to you?" Sinéad wanted to know.

"Please," Bernie translated.

"What an odd thing to say!" Sinéad exclaimed, but Bernie shook her head.

"That's what you say in Russian when somebody thanks you. It's like saying 'you're welcome'."

"So who's sleeping where?" Gráinne asked, looking around the small room with its three divan beds, armchair, small table and bare walls.

"I don't care once I haven't to share with Amanda," Bernie cried and, indeed, she was happy enough to take the bed in the corner by the door and give the others the ones on either side of the window.

"There's not much room for clothes," Sinéad said, looking at the three shelves and small hanging space in the little wall press.

"Can't we keep most things in the cases under our beds?" Gráinne replied, as she tucked her nightie under the pillow. "Mine will just about fit."

But while Sinéad and Gráinne were settling their things in the press, Bernie still stood looking out of the open window. The imposing three-storey building opposite ran the whole length of the street. Half-way down its style changed, becoming modern with bright stained glass windows on the upper level, with pictures of groups of dancers. There was a constant traffic of young people in twos and threes crossing the road between the old part of the building and the one they were in.

"That must be the school across the road," Bernie said.

At that moment she saw Willie and Larry appear from directly beneath her and cross the road towards the big heavy door opposite. At the top of the steps they turned and looked back. Bernie waved to them and, seeing her at the open window, they beckoned.

"They want us to go over," Bernie told the other two, adding – as Willie made extravagant mimed gestures of eating with hands to mouth – "I think there must be food going."

At the mention of food the others dropped everything and the three hurried out on to the landing just as Betty came flying down the stairs from the floor above.

"There's a meal ready in the canteen," she said. "Are you coming?"

"Where's the canteen?" Bernie asked.

"Follow me," Betty laughed, as she hurried on down the lower flight of stairs.

Bernie was glad she had found a friendly guide who spoke English but, to be sure of managing on her own in future, she took careful note of everything. The double glass doors a few feet in from the heavy wooden outside one crashed shut, she noticed, if you just let go of them instead of closing them carefully. To the right was a waiting area with two battered sofas, two armchairs and a table surrounded by four upright chairs, while straight

27

ahead up four steps was a lobby leading to a corridor, divided from the waiting area by an iron trellis patterned with musical notes and clefs. To the left, behind another grille, there was a cloakroom and outside it sat a little old woman who greeted Betty like a long-lost granddaughter. Betty said something to her in Russian and pointed to each of the others in turn, saying their names.

"*Zdravstvooeetya*," Bernie said, when her turn came and the old woman purred like a cat and patted her on the cheek.

"She loves it when you talk to her," Betty told her as she led them to the left along a passage and to the right again. "She used to teach dancing herself until she got too old. Now she just sits there all day long, making sure no one nicks anything out of the cloakrooms and telling visitors where to go. You'll be a favourite now because you said hullo to her."

Bernie realised she would probably have found the canteen without a guide from the babble of voices coming from the open door on their left. Even so, all the tables were not full and she saw after a second that only the Irish were there.

"The others have eaten already," Betty explained. "It's just for us because we got here late."

Then she hurried over to greet a fair-haired woman in a white coat who was handing out plates of food. Again she got a warm greeting and Bernie decided that either Betty was especially popular or this was the friendliest place she had ever been. Then she noticed Amanda, already sitting at a table with Barbara and her three travelling companions, looking at the plate in front of her as if it contained a large black slug.

"What are we getting?" she asked Willie, as she joined him in the queue at the serving hatch.

"Russian bangers and mash," he grinned and, as she got her own plate, she saw that it contained a pile of rather watery-looking potato, surrounded by slices of the same fatty red sausage she had had on the train.

At that moment Richard and Michael strolled into the canteen together. Michael had a sour look on his face and, even though there was room at some of the tables where people were already sitting, as soon as they had collected their food he led the way over to a fourth table, where they sat on their own.

"Why's Michael got a puss on him?" Bernie asked.

"He's fed up having to share a room with us," Larry told her. "He thought he could get a double with Richard, but Richard's with the two Russians he was sharing with last year, when he was the only Irish boy here."

"I didn't know there were any doubles," Bernie said.

"I think they're mostly doubles," Willie told her. "Your pal Amanda's in a double with Barbara and the second year girls are in doubles."

"Poor Barbara," Bernie said, "having to share with Amanda."

"Maybe Amanda would rather be with people her own age too," Willie suggested, but Bernie shook her head.

"Don't you know she's only delighted to be with someone outa the top class at Byrne's," she said, "but Michael must be real mad having to share with beginners."

"I've only done class for fifteen months," Larry argued, "but Willie's no beginner."

"I only started three months ahead of you," Willie protested. "We're both beginners next to Michael."

"And he's throwing all sorts of shapes about it," Gráinne pointed out. "Look at him!"

"Who could we ask about sharing?" Michael was demanding, as the others glanced over at him.

"What's the use when there's no double free?" Richard asked. "And anyway I'm happy enough sharing with Rudi. It's Misha that gets up my nose. He won't play along with anything."

"Couldn't I swap with him then?" Michael suggested.

"If he agreed I suppose you could," Richard shrugged, "provided the two in your room were willing to go along with it."

"Leave that to me!" Michael told him grimly. "That pair will be willing to have the devil himself rather than me by the time I'm finished with them!"

Character Class

"*Eeee – raas, eeee – dva, eeee – tree, eeee – chatiree*," the teacher called out and Willie instinctively responded to the familiar sound although the words were different. For the long drawn-out "eeee" sounded so exactly like the long drawn out "aaaand" that he was used to that, no matter what had been said next, he would have taken it to be a count of four.

As he went through his *pliés*, *port de bras*, *battements tendus*, *ronds de jambe* and *developpés* in the small corner studio looking out on the river and the Ural Mountains beyond, the hand under the chin to lift the head or the jab between the shoulder blades to straighten the back felt much the same too. Language problems would obviously not be a major worry, though he resolved to work hard at his Russian classes so he could understand all the little comments the teacher made.

He was at the *barre* facing the big windows between Larry and Michael, who was disgusted at being started in the same class as they were, the more so because Richard, in his second year there, was in a senior class. The privileged position facing the mirror had already been taken by the five Russian boys. One of these, a slim, fair-haired boy about his own age with high cheekbones and laughing eyes, had smiled at Willie when he arrived and pointed to himself.

"Misha," he had said and then, pointing to Willie, asked, "You?"

"Willie," Willie had told him.

"Vili," Misha had repeated.

Then he had picked up an orange plastic watering-can from the corner of the room and gestured to Willie to follow him as he walked to the door. He led Willie to a sink with a cold water tap, where he filled the can.

"You," he said again to Willie.

"You mean, next time I do it?" Willie asked and Misha grinned.

Maybe he was just glad to have found someone lower in the pecking order than himself to do the chores, but Willie decided immediately that he liked him. He followed him back to the corner studio and watched as he watered the smooth wooden floor around the *barre* areas to make it less slippery. When it was time to move away from the *barre*, Willie fetched the watering-can himself and sprinkled the centre of the floor. It was strange, but somehow performing this simple task made him feel that he was already a fully paid-up member of the class.

The Russians lined up in front so the Irish boys had only to copy them if they were in doubt as to what exactly they were supposed to be doing. As the class continued Willie was glad he had chosen to stand behind Misha for, whenever either of them made a hash of anything, they exchanged sympathetic grins. After class, Willie tapped Misha on the arm.

"This is my friend Larry," he said. "Larry, this is Misha."

"Hi, Misha," Larry said.

"La-ri," Misha repeated gravely, shaking hands in such a formal way that they all laughed.

As they pulled their T-shirts on over their leotards Willie noticed how the Russian boys all rolled theirs up to just under their armpits, giving them a rather dashing appearance. Carefully he copied them and Misha nodded his approval.

"Roll up your T-shirt, Larry," Willie told him. "All the others do."

And, when Larry did as he was told, Misha gave his usual wide grin.

For all the new Irish students the next few days passed in a blur of classes, confusion and unfamiliar faces. Like Michael, Amanda had been disgusted to find that all the new girls had been put into the same class to begin with. As soon as they entered the large, blue-painted studio with its twenty chandeliers, she had separated herself from Bernie and the Cunningham cousins by taking the last place at the *barre* behind Barbara and the other three Irish girls on the far side of the studio where large windows looked down on to the street. The long wall opposite the mirror was already occupied by five Russians and one Japanese girl, so Bernie joined Gráinne and Sinéad at the shorter *barre* between the door from the landing and the one leading into the adjoining studio, where one small Japanese girl stood all by herself.

"Hullo," Bernie said to her. "I mean *zdravstvooeetya.*"

"Velly solly, English speaking bad," the girl answered,

smiling apologetically, "but better than Lussian. Only begin learning Lussian now."

"Me too," Bernie grinned, "and your English is a lot better than my Japanese. The only Japanese word I know is *sayonara* and my Russian's not much better! My name's Bernie. What's yours?"

"Shiori," the girl told her, but before she could say more their teacher arrived with the accompanist.

She was a tall, red-haired woman wearing a black skirt and purple cardigan and, even before the end of class, Bernie knew her worries had been needless, for the teacher gave her the same feeling that Madame Chumakova had done of knowing exactly what she was doing. She seemed to have very little English but, after they had finished the exercises at the *barre* and were doing small *enchainements*, she had called out *"Kharashoh!"* as Bernie finished. Bernie flushed with delight. Even had it not been one of the few Russian words she knew, the approving tone of voice would have made its meaning clear. She had made a good start.

Over the next few days her first impressions were confirmed. Their ballet teacher expected a lot of them, but was quick with praise when it was deserved. Bernie began to look forward to ballet classes, but her first piano lesson was another matter. As she walked between the rows of numbered doors her footsteps became slower and slower. From each door came the sound of different piano pieces: all, it seemed to Bernie, played by accomplished pianists. From one floated a John Field nocturne, from another a bouncy Russian folk dance, from a third passages from a Rachmaninov concerto. How could she ever make beautiful sounds like those? She pictured herself stumbling through boring exercise pieces, constantly hitting wrong notes, or spending years playing nothing but scales.

She suddenly realised she had reached the door with the right number. From inside came a tune she knew very well indeed. It was Tchaikovsky's "Dance of the Little Swans." She had heard it played again and again during that first summer school. It was the music that had been the start of all her hopes. Whoever it was was playing her tune. She tapped on the door and walked in.

At the piano sat Betty and, watching her play, a dark-haired woman with her hair in a bun. As Bernie hung back just inside the doorway the piece came to an end.

"Kharashoh!" said the dark-haired woman, before launching into a flood of Russian which Bernie couldn't understand.

Betty nodded and put away her music before turning and seeing Bernie.

"Hi!" she smiled. "Come on in."

"You are Bernadette Flood?" the teacher asked, consulting a list.

Bernie nodded.

"I'm afraid I never learned the piano," she mumbled. "I'd love to be able to play like Betty."

Betty laughed.

"That shouldn't take long. I'm not very good. I only started learning when I came out here a year ago."

"Pozhalsta, Betty," the teacher said. *"Ya nye poneemahyoo."*

Apologising, Betty translated what Bernie had said

and her reply. Smiling, the teacher motioned Bernie to sit down at the piano.

"*Doh zveedaneeyah,*" Betty said as she went out and Bernie, glad to have heard another phrase she knew, called out "goodbye" in Russian too.

Then the teacher took her hands and looked at them, noting the long extended fingers.

"*Kharashoh,*" she said again.

Bernie thought it great that she could find something good before she had even started. Then the teacher extended her hands over the piano keys.

Bernie stretched out her fingers as she had seen keyboard players do at home, but the teacher shook her head. She took Bernie's hands, one by one, in her own, forcing the palms upwards so that the fingers pointed downward at a sharper angle. Then she nodded.

Something suddenly clicked into place in Bernie's head. Since Russian dance technique was different, maybe Russian piano-playing technique was different too. Carefully keeping her hands in the position in which the teacher had placed them, she found that by the end of the hour she could already play a simple little melody.

Sinéad stood in the doorway of the little room at the foot of the small flight of stairs leading down from the top floor studios and stared. She felt like a small child staring into a sweet shop window, but it was not sweets that were stacked in rows along the shelves lining the walls. Red as any lollipop or boiled sweet they might be, but these were shoes. You had only to look at them to see the swirl of brightly-coloured skirts and hear the

. . . it was not sweets that were stacked in rows along the shelves lining the walls . . . these were shoes.

stamping as they beat the ground in a tempestuous Russian folk dance. And now she was to be fitted with a pair of her own for character class.

The small room was crowded with people trying on shoes. Gráinne had pushed her way in and was already trying on a pair, but Sinéad stood, dazed, until the elderly lady in the dark grey skirt beckoned her. Sinéad went over to her and the lady looked at her feet and smiled.

"Malenkee!" she said, holding up her two hands with the palms facing inwards as if to suggest just how small they were.

Sinéad nodded. She was small for her age anyway, but she did have really small feet. The lady reached up on to a high shelf and took down a pair of small character shoes so red and shiny they made Sinéad think of the red apples her Aunt Nan used to polish on her apron. She sat down on the floor and slipped her feet into them. They fitted as if they had been made for her and she was excited by the feel of the soft worn leather, wanting to stamp and twirl. Suddenly she remembered the story of the red shoes and how the girl who had bought them could neither take them off nor stop dancing.

"Kharashoh," the lady nodded approvingly.

She opened a big book and wrote something in it before handing the biro to Sinéad to sign her name against it. Sinéad would have liked to keep the shoes on, but character class was still more than an hour away. She turned to look for Gráinne and found her kneeling on one knee in the passage with one shoe on and the other in her hand.

"Will you be long?" Sinéad asked her.

"All day at this rate," Gráinne said. "The right foot feels fine, but the left one's too tight to dance in. The last person to wear these must have had one foot bigger than the other."

"Unless you have," Sinéad told her. "Anyway, I've got mine and there's no room to wait here. I'll see you across the road."

Cradling the beautiful red shoes in her arms she followed the corridor round to the main staircase and ran down the two flights of stairs to the lobby. As she crossed the street she saw Larry and Willie, sitting on the steps leading up to the door of the hostel.

"Are you so wrecked you can't climb the steps without a sit-down?" she teased, but for once Willie didn't smile.

"We're having a council of war," he said.

"Funny place to have it," Sinéad commented. "What's wrong with your room?"

"Everything," Larry told her. "That's why we're having a council of war. Michael's gotta go."

"Or we will," Willie added. "It's down to him or us."

"Why? What's he done?" Sinéad asked in surprise.

Michael had never been a friend. He was a good bit older than her for a start, but he had been kind enough in a condescending sort of way.

"He was impossible from the minute we got here," Willie explained. "You know the ridiculous way he goes on about his clothes? Well, he took ever bit of hanging space and most of the shelves too. Not that I'm fussy about where I put my things, but then he complains I'm making the place untidy if I leave stuff out on the chair."

"And every night he washes something and hangs it up on a hanger by the window to dry out overnight," Larry said.

"I know if you leave them downstairs in the drying room they're likely to get nicked," Willie added, "but if it's windy you've got this wet thing flapping and dripping all over everything."

"But never over *his* things," Larry pointed out.

"And this morning I found my T-shirt as wet as if he'd washed that too," Willie finished angrily.

"Have you tried talking to him?" Sinéad asked.

"He only gives out about how untidy and dirty *we* are," Larry told her, "and then he slams out of the room."

"And I think he *meant* his socks to drip on my T-shirt," Willie added, "because he hung them up after we were asleep and he could easily have moved the chair out of the way."

"That's awful!" Sinéad said. "What are you going to do?"

"I dunno," Larry told her. "I wish he could share with Richard. I know it's what he wants and it would get him off our backs."

"I don't care if he sleeps on the street," Willie cried, "but he can't go on sharing with us. We'll have to think of something."

Making sympathetic noises, Sinéad stepped over them and went on up to her room. Bernie was sitting on her bed, writing a letter. She looked up as Sinéad came in.

"Did anyone get a letter from home yet?" she asked.

Sinéad shook her head.

"Don't think so. Me and Gráinne didn't anyway. But I suppose letters take ages to get here from Ireland and we haven't been here long. Gráinne said she might try 'phoning on Sunday if we haven't heard by then."

"We've no 'phone at home," Bernie said, "but I'm writing to ask Mammy to 'phone me."

"Betty said you often have to wait for an hour or more to get through," Sinéad told her. "It won't be easy for her to ring from a 'phone box, will it?"

"Then I'll tell her to ring from Madigans," Bernie said. "They've a public 'phone in the lounge."

A burst of laughter from beneath the open window made Sinéad turn and look out. Willie and Larry were no longer sitting on the steps. Instead Gráinne, her character shoes in her hand, was there with two Russian boys. Considering that they had very little English and Gráinne only a few words of Russian, they seemed to be managing very well indeed.

Sinéad felt a tinge of jealousy. Suddenly she remembered the Youth Dance Festival in Cork, when Gráinne had disappeared after the céilí with Mick Furlong. It had been the only time there had ever been a coldness between them. When it came to boys, it seemed that there was a whole side to her cousin that she didn't really know. With Gráinne living in Cork and herself in Dublin, they'd never been around boys any time they were together. It suddenly struck Sinéad now that it could be lonely here if Gráinne made new friends of her own. But she soon forgot such thoughts during character class.

She had always looked forward to character class during Madame Chumakova's two summer schools but now, working with Russians who seemed to have their own folk dance in their blood, made it even more exciting. Although she had adapted fast to ballet she felt sure she would never be as good at it as Bernie and Gráinne. But at character class she could outshine them both. Russian, Spanish, Hungarian and Polish folk dances were quite different from the jigs and hornpipes for which she had won so many medals, but there seemed to be something all folk dancing had in common. Soon her small figure was stamping and twirling as adroitly as the Russians.

Another thing about character class was that the class was mixed. With ballet the girls were on their own until they started to do duet class in their second year, but in character class they had boys for partners in dances like the *czarda*s and Sinéad was paired with a fair-haired Russian boy with high cheekbones and laughing eyes out of Larry and Willie's class. He could already do the *gopak* like an expert and Sinéad was delighted to have him for a partner. Was it only because they were the shortest couple that they were put out in the front to lead?

Flushed with success as class ended, Sinéad looked around for Gráinne, but she was still at the far end of the studio, laughing and joking with her partner, a tall, dark-haired boy who had been with her on the hostel steps earlier. As Sinéad wondered whether or not to wait for her, Willie and Larry came over.

"You two were deadly," Willie said.

Sinéad's partner looked puzzled.

"Kharashoh!" Willie translated, giving him a thumbs-up sign.

42

"You were real cool, Misha," Larry nodded.

Misha gave one of his wide grins.

"Cool cat, is OK, yes?"

"Misha?" Sinéad echoed. "Is that his name?"

Misha gave her a funny little mock bow.

"You?" he asked.

"That's Sinéad," Larry told him.

"Shin-ade," Misha repeated, bowing again.

"Come on," Larry said pulling on his T-shirt. "I want a shower and by then it should be time to eat."

"I hope it's sausage again this evening," Willie said, swinging his boots over his shoulder. "That was the boniest chicken I ever saw at lunch. It either walked here on its own two feet or it died of old age."

"I'd say it died of hunger," Larry grinned, as they left the studio with Misha, "and we'll be lucky if we don't do the same!"

By the time Bernie got to the canteen she found the babble louder than usual. A mixture of suppressed excitement and unease seemed to be spreading from table to table.

"What's going on?" she asked Willie, who was already tucking in.

"I dunno," Willie told her. "The woman who met us at the station came in just now and made an announcement, but I didn't understand what she said."

"Betty's real good at the Russian," Bernie said. "Why don't I ask her? Don't let anyone nick my hamburger."

She was making her way across the crowded canteen to where Betty sat when Amanda reached out and gripped her arm.

"Did you hear the news?" she whispered

dramatically. "We've all to get injections in the morning. Loads of people in town are sick and the doctor says it's diphtheria!"

"Diphtheria?" Bernie echoed stupidly.

"And that's fatal," Amanda continued, making the most of it. "Your throat gets real sore and you can't swallow anything so you'd die of the hunger only for you can't breathe so you're already dead from lack of oxygen!"

The Dying Swan

"Don't mind her," said Betty reassuringly from across the table. "Diphtheria can be cured with antibiotics if it's got soon enough. Anyway, no one in the school has it and, if we all get our shots, no one's going to."

"We'll only have sore arms from the needle so we can't dance," Amanda complained. "I hate getting jabs."

"That's right, look on the bright side!" Betty chuckled, winking at Bernie. "There's nothing like a good laugh to cheer us all up."

So Bernie went back to the others grinning.

Next day her left arm was a little sore after the injection, but not enough to stop her doing class. It got hot and throbbed a bit that night, but she was far too tired for it to keep her awake long and by the following day she had forgotten about it. Her mind was far too full of the steps of the "Garland Dance" from The Sleeping Beauty, which they were learning in repertory class. And when she wasn't thinking about that she was worrying about the lack of news from home. When one day she saw Amanda with a letter in her hand, even the fact that it was Amanda didn't stop her running after her looking for news of Dublin.

"Did you get that letter today?" she asked.

Amanda nodded.

"It's from Mammy," she said.

"Does she say how classes are going?" Bernie asked eagerly. "I was thinking only yesterday about Eileen and Kylie and the rest of them doing class in the Molesworth Hall as if we had never left."

"The autumn classes hadn't even started when she wrote," Amanda told her. "The letter took ages to get here. Look at the postmark."

"But that's only a few days after we left Dublin!" Bernie exclaimed, turning the battered envelope over in her hand. "Why did it take so long?"

"It's been opened," Amanda said. "It must have been, because Mammy says she enclosed something to get me a few extras and there's nothing in it."

"That's desperate!" Bernie exclaimed. "But even at home it's dodgy sending cash in a letter."

"How else *can* you send it here?" Amanda complained. "You can't send cheques or postal orders. The only thing you can do is send dollars."

Standing between Shiori and Gráinne, each with one leg up on the *barre* gently stretching, Bernie told them about Amanda's letter as they warmed up for class that morning.

"This happen also to my fliend Fukuyo," Shiori said. "I tell palents. They hide dollars in packet of seaweed soup!"

"Dollar soup! I like it!" laughed Gráinne. "Betty says you can ring home on Sundays from the post office, so I might give it a try Sunday. And I'll tell them if they're sending anything worth nicking to make sure to hide it."

"It's a good idea," Bernie said. "They seem to give letters from abroad a going-over. It's a wonder they didn't nick the soup."

"Not evlybody like seaweed soup," Shiori told her.

"I don't blame them. It sounds really yucky!" Bernie said but, as Shiori shook her head laughing, the arrival of teacher and accompanist put an end to further conversation.

In the lobby on the way back to the hostel after class, they overtook Misha. He gave them his usual grin but Sinéad thought he seemed in poor form.

"You look a bit down," she said.

Misha seemed puzzled, so she tried again.

"Is anything wrong?" she asked.

"Not happy in room," he told her, shifting awkwardly from one foot to the other. "Boys make games I not like."

Now it was Sinéad's turn to look puzzled, but Shiori

immediately put a hand on his shoulder and spoke forcefully.

"You go to office now. Say you want other loom."

Misha shrugged unhappily.

"But where I sleep?"

"I know what you'll do," Sinéad cried. "You can swap with Michael."

"He'd be only delighted," Bernie agreed. "Isn't he always hanging around with Richard and Rudi?"

"And I know Willie and Larry would much rather share with you," Sinéad added. "Michael's driving them mad."

"Let's go and find them," Gráinne suggested.

So after character class, Misha, Willie and Larry tapped on the door of the administrator's office on the first floor.

"What will we say?" Larry whispered.

"I talk," Misha told him, and he certainly did.

Willie and Larry couldn't understand much of what he was saying but, although he stammered a little and got pink in the face, he said a great deal. The tall woman kept saying, *"Da, da,"* and then turned to Willie and Larry.

"You like also?" she asked.

"Oh yes, please!" Willie said, and Larry added, *"Da! Da!"*, nodding vigorously to emphasise the point.

The administrator said something else to Misha and he stood up.

"Spaceboh," he said to her and, to the others, "Is good. We go now."

"Spaceboh!" Larry and Willie chorused gratefully and followed Misha out of the office.

"What did you say to her?" Larry asked, but Misha only answered, "She say tell Michael, Richard and Rudi go see her now."

If the interview with the administrator was in any way unpleasant, Michael showed no sign of it when he returned to the hostel. In fact he seemed triumphant.

"After class I'll be moving out my gear," he told Willie and Larry grandly. "I'm going to share with people who don't leave smelly tights on their beds or junk piled on the only chair."

Feeling equally triumphant, Willie smiled angelically.

"I hope you'll be very happy," he said politely, winking at Larry who doubled up with suppressed laughter.

After class they helped Misha carry his clothes down from the top floor and were amazed at the space they had now Michael's things were gone.

"We needn't keep our gear on the chair any more," Larry pointed out. "There's room on the shelves for everything now."

"We can unpack at last," Willie agreed.

"Is OK?" Misha asked, holding a brightly-coloured poster advertising the Kirov Ballet against the wall above his bed.

"Deadly!" Larry cried. "It brightens up the room, doesn't it, Willie? If we can get a few more posters we could put them up on either side of the press."

"Hey, that looks great!" Bernie called out as she passed the open door on her way to the shower. "And the room's much neater-looking."

"Everything's better without Michael," Larry told her.

"But you've still got a Michael, a Russian one," Bernie

pointed out. "Didn't you know Misha's short for Michael?"

"In Russian is Mikhail," Misha told him, smiling.

"That's gas!" Larry said.

"We have to celebrate this," Willie shouted. "Let's have a party!"

Larry looked embarrassed.

"I'm a bit short of the readies," he said, "and I don't imagine Misha has it to throw around either."

"Then we'll have one as soon as my Dad sends me a few bob like he promised," Willie told him. "But I've enough now to buy the three of us Coke. Is there somewhere we could go, Misha?"

"Not understand," Misha said.

"Is there a café anywhere near?" Willie asked.

"Is Dragon Café, near Opera House," Misha told him. "Is good."

"If you mean the one in 25th October Street, it was closed the other morning," Larry said.

"Opens later," Misha assured him. "When peoples finish work. Also on Sunday."

"Right," Willie said. "We'll go next Sunday."

Sunday was the one day when they had some time to themselves. There were no classes and they could sleep on for a while in the morning, get their washing done and explore the town. The Russian State Choreographic Institute was in the old part of town and though the big houses had now all become civic offices or were used by companies of one kind or another, they still had a gracious look in the autumn sunshine.

"You should get out and see the place while you can," Betty had told Gráinne. "It's at its best in

50

September. Soon winter will be here and everything will be under ice and snow for months on end."

But this Sunday Gráinne had made up her mind to try to 'phone home. She had done her sums, worked out the time difference and decided that if she put a call through about midday she could be sure her parents wouldn't have gone out to Mass, even if it took more than an hour to get the call through. She would run the risk of waking everyone at seven in the morning if she got through right away, but that seemed unlikely to happen, from what Betty said. In any case, they would probably be nice about it in the circumstances.

Of course the afternoon would have been the best time to get them but, with the time difference, by Sunday dinner-time in Cork the post office would be closed for the night. So, after she and Sinéad had had a good lie-in and washed their tights, leotards and undies, they both set out for the post office.

They cut across the park in front of the opera house, glancing at it as they passed. Facing up the broad central path, with a statue on a pedestal and seats on either side, its white and gold splendour sparkled in the sunlight. Five storeys high, with fifteen long windows between its eight pillars, it was topped by a magnificent pediment. Of course it was small compared with the Bolshoi, which they had seen on their brief tour of Moscow, but it still retained something of the splendour it had had during the reign of the Tsars.

"Isn't it beautiful?" Sinéad cried. "I do wish we had an opera house in Dublin."

"We have one in Cork," Gráinne boasted.

"Not a beautiful one like this," Sinéad retorted and

for once, proud though she was of Cork, Gráinne had no real answer.

"Well, it was built in a hurry on the cheap when the old one burnt down," was the best she could manage.

"Maybe we could get to see a show here some day," Sinéad suggested and Gráinne nodded.

"Oh, we will. Betty says they have lots of ballet as well as opera, and Madame likes us to see as much as we can."

In the post office Gráinne booked a call to Cork, having asked the ever-obliging Betty to write down any words she might need. Having already learned to count up to twenty, she assumed she would be able to understand how many hours delay there would be. When it came to the point, however, she could make no sense of the operator's words. Hoping they wouldn't be there all day, she settled down to wait.

Meanwhile, Bernie sat on her bed darning her point shoes. What with Russian lessons, piano lessons, ballet, repertoire and character classes, to say nothing of the hurly-burly of meals and school and hostel life in general, she normally had no time to feel homesick. Now, alone in the unusual quiet of their room, it suddenly hit her. She knew it was stupid. It was only a few weeks since she had kissed her mother goodbye at Dublin Airport, but she had never been away from home for more than a weekend before and, in spite of herself, she found tears dripping on to the point shoes in her lap. In her head she could hear her mother's voice as clearly as if she were in the room with her.

"Bernie, love," the voice said, "don't take on so! Aren't you doing what you've been wanting to do since you were a babby?"

But hearing her voice in her head was no substitute for feeling her mother's arms around her. She would even have been glad to hear her father giving out to her. She knew exactly what he would say.

"Will yous look at her? Crying, if yous don't mind, an' she nearly takin' the bit outa our mouths to get herself out there!"

It wouldn't have been so bad, Bernie thought, if Eileen had been there too. Even Kylie would have made it feel more like home, though having a younger sister dragging out of her would have been a bore at times. But now she was so homesick she would even have welcomed her brothers jeering at her for "doing the Dying Swan" or the sight of her older sister Imelda sitting on the bed opposite removing her curlers as she gave out to her.

Still, crying wouldn't bring them any nearer. It was only making her throat sore. She must get her second point shoe darned and then put a few stitches in her practice costume. Anyway, Gráinne and Sinéad would be back soon and she mustn't let them see her crying. She blew her nose vigorously and went back to her darning.

Gráinne and Sinéad, however, were still in the post office. One hour and fifteen minutes had passed and they were getting worried.

"Are you *sure* she booked the call?" Sinéad asked for the third time.

"Of course I'm sure," Gráinne replied indignantly.

"But if you didn't understand what she said to you . . ." Sinéad began.

"She was only saying something about there being a delay, I expect," Gráinne interrupted.

"I don't see how you know that if you didn't understand her," Sinéad pointed out. "She might have been saying, 'All lines to Ireland are out of order because of the storm'!"

"What storm?" Gráinne demanded. "There hasn't been a storm."

"There could have been one in Ireland," Sinéad told her. "There often is in October. Or she might have said, 'There's a four hour delay on all overseas calls'."

"I'd have understood if she said 'four'," Gráinne argued, "or any other number of hours for that matter."

"All the same, I'd be happier if we knew what she did say," Sinéad argued. "We're going to miss lunch if we hang on here much longer."

But at that moment the girl behind the counter called out her name.

"*Da!*" Gráinne cried eagerly, running up to the counter. "*Da, da, spaceboh!*"

She paid for the call and waited by the 'phone booth in a frenzy of impatience. Suddenly the 'phone rang and she dived on it.

"Mammy! . . . No, no, nothing's wrong. I'm fine and so's Sinéad. Why didn't you write? . . . Well, I didn't get it. Did you get mine? . . . Only Friday? But I wrote the day after we got here, like I promised. Is Da OK? . . . Yeah, well, listen, Mammy, in case I get cut off. Sinéad wants to talk to you too . . . Yeah, she's right beside me, but first there's something important . . ."

By the time she had given her mother the 'phone number of the hostel and arranged that she would put through a call there the minute she got back from Mass every Sunday and would tell her sister-in-law to do the same from Dublin, Gráinne's money had run out, but both girls felt happier. To hear someone's voice, however faint or distorted, seemed to bring them nearer than any amount of letters.

"We'll have to stay near the 'phone every Sunday afternoon," Gráinne told Sinéad, "but if she rings straight after Mass and Aunt Phil does the same, one or other of them's sure to get through before 6:45 even if the delay's more than two hours."

"Why 6:45?" Sinéad asked.

"So we can make the Opera House by seven if we're going, stupid!" Gráinne said. "And she's sorry she didn't get to talk to you but she sends her love and she'll ring Aunt Phil straight after Mass. She was talking to her only yesterday and she and your Dad and Niall are all fine."

"Great," Sinéad cried. "I don't mind so much now about missing lunch."

"Tell you what," Gráinne said. "Why don't we go to that café we passed on the way back from the river last Sunday? I'm sure I've enough money to get us both something and it couldn't be worse than that awful scraggy bit of chicken we got last week."

"That would be deadly," Sinéad cried, "and I've a few roubles I could put to it. But will we ever make them understand what we want?"

"Can't we always point?" Gráinne shrugged.

So, after cutting back across the park to the corner of their own street, they turned left off it along 25th October Street.

When they weren't back in time for lunch, Bernie went across to the canteen by herself. She collected her potatoes, *kasha* and pickled cabbage from the hatch and joined Willie, Larry and Misha, who had almost finished theirs. She hoped they wouldn't notice that her eyes were still rather puffy, but they were full of their own plans and took little notice of her.

As soon as she began to eat, however, she found it hurt her to swallow. She had really managed to make her throat awfully sore, she thought. She mashed up the potato in gravy and ate that, picking at the rest, for even the *kasha* was too lumpy for her to swallow. It was so unusual for anybody not to demolish everything, however far from tempting it might be, that Willie was quick to notice when she pushed her plate away with food still on it.

"Are you sick or something?" he asked. "You hardly touched your *kasha*."

"Have it if you want," Bernie said. "My throat's too sore to swallow."

Now they were all looking at her.

"You look a bit under the weather," Larry said. "Maybe you should lie down for a while."

At the table behind them Barbara Jordan turned to look too.

"What's wrong?" she asked.

"My throat's a bit sore, that's all," Bernie told her, wishing she had stayed away from the canteen. "I must be getting a cold or something."

Amanda, sitting beside her room-mate, spun around.

"You'd better tell someone at once!" she cried. "You have to see a doc right away, because it's sure to be the start of diphtheria and we don't all want to get it off you!"

The Nutcracker

In the end it was Betty who did the telling because she had enough Russian to explain. She had outlined Bernie's symptoms to Anna who, at a boarding school in the west, would have been called Matron but was, like everyone else at the State Choreographic Institute, a former dancer. In addition to teaching, however, she had particular responsibility for the health of the students. She had taken one look at Bernie, sent her to bed and called the doctor.

Lying there on her own with nothing to do but think how homesick she was and worry in case she really *was* getting diphtheria, Bernie soon began to feel a great deal worse. It was bad enough being thousands of miles from home, she thought, but being ill when you were thousands of miles away was worse. And if it really *was* diphtheria they would send her to hospital.

She remembered how she had dreaded going back to the Meath Hospital after the doctor in casualty had said she would never dance again. Russian hospitals might be even worse. She thought of all the stories about shortages of medicines and equipment. She was imagining herself having to have an operation without anaesthetic by the time the doctor arrived.

He was a stocky, broad-shouldered man with fair hair

and a reassuring smile. He took Bernie's temperature, checked her blood pressure, sounded her chest and back and examined her throat. Then he said something to Anna, who had been hovering in the background, and her look of relief told Bernie it was not diphtheria.

"Betty come," Anna told her as the doctor gave her a reassuring pat on the shoulder and the two of them left the room.

Within minutes there was a tap on the door and Betty came in and sat down on the bed.

"You haven't got any sort of infection," she told Bernie. "Your sore throat is from pollution. There's a problem here with all the factories in the new part of town. The doctor left a prescription and I'm going to the pharmacy now to get it made up. The doctor says whenever the wind's from the west, like it's been for the past few days, you should wear a mask."

"A mask!" Bernie echoed in horror, thinking of the sort of masks they had all bought at Hallowe'en when they were younger.

"It's usual here in the winter," Betty told her, "especially when the snow clouds are low in the sky and the smoke all blows downwards. People tie scarves over their mouths and noses whenever they go out. Anything to keep out the pollution. Isn't it a lot better than getting a sore throat?"

Bernie nodded eagerly.

"It would have been real scary to have diphtheria," she said.

"Take no notice of that eejit Amanda," Betty told her. "Why would you get diphtheria when you had your shots like everyone else? Amanda was just enjoying the drama. She would probably have liked us all to be threatened with pneumonic plague. Well, I'd better go and get your prescription made up. I'm sorry to leave you on your own. What happened the others?"

"They went out ages ago to try and 'phone Cork," Bernie said. "They oughta be back long ago. I hope they're OK."

"Of course, I remember now," Betty said. "They asked me to write down what they should say to the operator. Don't worry if they're back late. 'Phoning Ireland can take for ever. They'll just be gnawing the post office counter with the hunger."

As it happened she was quite wrong. At that moment Gráinne and Sinéad were sitting at a table in the café leading off the strangely bare, high-ceilinged shop in 25th October Street, hungrily sniffing the exciting smell coming from the far door every time it swung open. There was no menu, only a blackboard on the wall with words chalked up on it in Cyrillic script. They had started learning the Russian alphabet, but it was one thing to recognise letters when they were neatly printed and quite another when they were scrawled in someone's hurried handwriting in chalk. In any case, Gráinne thought, she probably wouldn't know the Russian words even if she could make out the letters.

There was a group of people at a corner table on the other side of the room and she wondered what they were having. It would be so much easier to point to one of their dishes and say *Dvar*, holding up two fingers at the same time to make sure they understood her. When the elderly woman who was serving brought a bottle to the corner table, however, and Gráinne turned to look as casually as she could, she realised they were only having coffee and vodka. If they had had a meal it was over by now.

Then the elderly woman came over to them for their order. Gráinne could only point vaguely at the blackboard. The woman went across to it and pointed to the top line.

"Should we say 'yes' and chance it?" Sinéad asked.

"And end up with vodka?" Gráinne countered. "Wouldn't that be smart?" She shook her head at the woman, who then pointed to the second line. Gráinne looked helpless. "I wish I knew the Russian for food," she said.

"*Myasa's* meat," Sinéad reminded her.

"So it is," Gráinne said, as the woman pointed to the third line.

"*Myasa?*" Gráinne suggested tentatively, but the woman shook her head, shrugging wearily.

By now the people at the corner table were watching the pantomime with amused expressions.

"It's no good," Gráinne said hopelessly. "We'll just have to go hungry."

She started to push her chair back from the table when suddenly the door from the shop swung open and in walked Willie, Larry and Misha. Never had Sinéad been happier to see anybody than she was to see her partner from character class just then. Jumping up she ran over to him.

"What can you get to eat in this place?" she cried.

Misha looked confused.

"Ice cream?" he suggested.

"D'you mean we can't get a proper meal?" Sinéad asked. "We missed lunch."

Misha understood the word "lunch".

"Soup?" he asked.

"Is that all?"

"Is good," he told her, noticing the disappointment in her face. "You have with bread. Is also cheese."

"OK," Gráinne said. "Soup, bread and cheese for both of us. Will you order it for us, Misha?"

Grinning, Misha spoke to the elderly woman, who nodded, smiling, and went out by the far door. Misha pulled over a chair from another table and sat down beside Sinéad as Willie and Larry took the two vacant chairs at their table.

"Did you miss lunch too?" Gráinne asked Larry.

"No," he told her, "but it was worse than usual today. Only *kasha* left over from breakfast with potato and cabbage. We came to get ices. Did you order them as well as the soup, Misha?"

"She go see what colour she have," Misha explained.

By the time the boys were attacking strawberry ices and the girls were tucking into two big bowls of steaming hot beetroot soup with thick cuts of bread, the little group had the look of a party.

"You like?" Misha asked Sinéad.

"Mmm!" she nodded. "It's a lot nicer than the beetroot soup we get at school. It's much thicker and the yoghurt on top is lovely with it."

"Is sour cream," Misha told her. "Soup has much vegetable: carrots, also onion and other one."

"I've found a chicken bone!" Gráinne cried, holding it up for him to see. "Look!"

"Once was made with whole chicken," Misha told her. "Also meat from bull. Sorry, now only bones. Is famous Russian dish. Called *borsch*."

"I'm glad we picked today to celebrate Misha moving in," Willie said. "The ices were really needed after that ghastly lunch."

"Not as glad as I am," Sinéad said fervently. "If you hadn't appeared we'd have gone hungry."

She pushed aside her soup spoon and mopped up the last of the *borsch* with her bread, before finishing that with the cheese.

"Also I am glad," Misha grinned. "Ice cream is good. New friends good too. You like ice cream, Sinéad?"

He held out a spoonful of his for her to try, but Sinéad hesitated.

"It's not fair to be eating yours," she protested. "Have we enough money for ice creams as well, Gráinne?"

"I don't know how much the soup is," Gráinne said. "Will this cover it, Misha?"

Misha looked at the notes Gráinne held out for his inspection.

"Is enough," he told her. "I go ask ice cream for you also."

As the days went by the new Irish students settled down into a routine. Their Russian improved quickly, especially Gráinne's, which was soon better even than Bernie's, although she had started ahead of the others because of the time she had put in at the Ilac Centre. But then Gráinne spent a great deal of her time hanging around with Russian boys who had very little English. Sinéad spent more and more of her time on her own. It seemed that her worst fears might be coming true. Then one day, when she was alone in the room, there was a tap on the door. When she opened it, Shiori stood there with a large package in her hand.

"I get plesent flom Yokohama," she said.

"More seaweed soup?" Sinéad asked.

"No seaweed," Shiori giggled. "This special cookie. You tly please?"

Sinéad hesitated. She didn't want to offend Shiori, but she had seen the other Japanese girls squeaking with excitement over a jar of something so black and slimy-looking that she had been afraid even to ask what it was. When Shiori held out the opened package, however, it seemed to be full of biscuits. The meals were still neither filling nor exciting and food was always welcome unless there was something really odd about it. There couldn't be much wrong with biscuits, even if they were Japanese.

Putting in her hand to take one she found it was sealed in its own little cellophane bag, which crackled as she tore it open. The biscuit inside, when she bit into it, was not like any biscuit she had ever tasted before. Crisp and shiny brown, it broke with a snap and tasted very salty but nice, in an odd sort of way. She took another bite. Then she discovered something strange. The more you ate, the more you wanted. She had broken open four of the little sealed bags almost before she realised it.

"They're deadly," she said. "What are they?"

"Velly special Japanese cookie," Shiori told her. "Velly good for health. Stop you getting sore thloat like Bernie."

"Thanks a million," Sinéad said. "I shouldn't have eaten so many on you."

"We have more tomollow," Shiori smiled. "Today

teacher ask if I like go to Opela House on Sunday with fliend. I tell her I ask my fliend Sinéad. You like go?"

"Oh, I'd love to," Sinéad cried. "The ballet company are doing *Nutcracker*, aren't they?"

Shiori nodded. "Teacher say we do *Nutclacker* soon so should see. I tell her tomollow you like come."

The visit to the Opera House was wonderful. The building was as splendid inside as out, all white and gold, with marble pillars and staircases. These were bare of any carpet but, from the brass rod fittings that were still in place at the sides of every step, Sinéad guessed they had once been covered with rich red carpet to match the rich red velvet curtain that hung over the door she had looked at so enviously because it led backstage.

She felt very grand as she tiptoed up one of the great staircases to the top tier of seats, close to the beautiful painted ceiling, so she could look down on all the people below and in the great box once used by the Tsar. As the light in the great chandelier dimmed and the spotlights came up on the heavy red velvet curtains, she found herself trembling with excitement. Surely, she thought, there could be nothing more wonderful than to dance there, to a theatre that was full, as it was today, with mothers and fathers and children of all ages, almost every seat filled with little family groups.

When the performance began she was dazzled by the wonderful costumes, the beautiful silver wigs worn by the women in the party scene and the splendid dancing. But most of all she was fascinated by the tiny figure of Clara, to whom the whole wonderful adventure happened, for she looked no bigger than herself.

But most of all she was fascinated by the tiny figure
of Clara, to whom the whole wonderful
adventure happened . . .

"D'you think she's really a child?" she whispered to Shiori, but Shiori shook her head.

"Velly small soloist with company," she whispered back, "but other childlen at party are flom gladuation class."

"You mean from the top class in *our* school?" Sinéad gasped. "Oh, I wish I was in the graduation class."

For the rest of the performance she kept thinking how wonderful it would be if one day she could be among that beautiful glittering throng. Almost drunk with the excitement of it all, she poured out her dreams to Shiori as they walked back across the park.

"This is my dleam also," Shiori told her, "but my palents say, 'Velly solly, too small'!"

"That's what my mother's always saying," Sinéad cried. "She worries all the time that I don't eat enough. She says if I don't eat how do I expect to grow? Her eyes would really pop if she saw the way I eat everything that's going here. I suppose she'd say it was hunger sauce. But no matter what I eat I never seem to grow any taller!"

"Madame say no need for girl to be tall," Shiori said. "For boy is important, but not for girl."

"I suppose she thinks we can always dance Clara," Sinéad laughed. "And the girl who danced the Sugar Plum Fairy wasn't very tall either."

"So we both work velly hard and gladuate into company together," Shiori told her.

And from then on, Sinéad didn't mind that Gráinne spent so much of her time fooling around with the boys. Now she had a friend of her own.

Bernie, on the other hand, had found no special

friend to take Eileen's place. She had more to worry about. Though her sore throat soon disappeared and she finally got a letter from home, she continued to have spells of homesickness on Sundays. She also worried about her progress, for she knew her mother would be a long time paying back the loan she had got from Ma Mulcahy to help send her to Russia. She was determined that none of her family would ever be able to say that the money had been wasted and this meant keeping fit enough to work hard throughout the exhausting schedule at the school. So she tied her headscarf over her mouth and nose every time she went out if the clouds were low in the sky or a wind blew from the west. She also worked so hard in class that their teacher called out *Kharashoh* more and more often.

Amanda was quick to notice this and resent it. Not that she and Bernie were much together outside class. At meal times or on Sundays Amanda spent most of her time with Barbara and the girls who had shared Barbara's compartment on the train and, whenever she got a food parcel from home, she certainly didn't share its contents with Bernie or the Cunninghams. She seemed to prefer any company to theirs and one day, to Bernie's surprise, she even spotted her with Michael and Richard. They were strolling back from town across the park, munching sweets, as if they had all been on some outing together, though Bernie supposed they could have met by chance in town.

But if she were spared Amanda's cutting remarks at other times, she got plenty of black looks during class and the more Bernie was praised, the worse it got, until Bernie actually felt relieved whenever Amanda herself won a word of approval. This she sometimes did, for her dancing was quite good, though she never seemed to put her heart into it or respond to the music as Bernie did.

Indeed, sometimes Bernie felt as if she and the music were one, delighting in having Sonya to accompany them on the piano in class instead of always having the same boring old tapes they had had at Miss Byrne's. And Sonya always played ballet music for the class instead of just banging out the rhythm, as they had done in Malahide.

One day it struck Bernie that there was another reason why Amanda didn't always look good dancing. She was beginning to put on weight. Of course that was a problem for all of them, with a diet consisting mainly of starchy food like *kasha*, bread and watery potatoes, or fatty soups and sausage, but Bernie suspected Amanda was filling up the cracks by stuffing herself with chocolate.

Nor was she the only one to notice the change in Amanda's appearance. One day Madame Chumakova came in towards the end of class. She herself taught the graduation class in the room leading off theirs and this morning had let them go early because they would be rehearsing later on with the State Ballet Company in the Opera House. Taking the opportunity to see how the first year students were getting on, she slipped in unnoticed from the door behind the piano and the first Bernie knew of her presence was when she heard her harsh voice call out, "*Kharashoh*, Bernie!" Flushing with delight as she finished her series of turns, Bernie thought how important for her future career Madame's good opinion was and rejoiced that, so far at least, she seemed to have her approval.

A few minutes later, however, she clutched the *barre* in horror as, waiting her turn at the *jetés*, she heard the harsh voice call, "Jump, Amanda, you fat pig! What is good of training without you have will to dance?"

Even though she was no friend of Amanda, Bernie felt sorry for her, thinking how she herself would have felt to have had such a roar directed at her, in front of the whole class. It seemed that Madame, who had shown her such kindness when she injured her back during the summer school, could also be cruel. But all pity for Amanda soon disappeared in the cut-throat competition that began during the next day's repertory class.

They had begun learning the Arabian Dance from the last act of *The Nutcracker* and rumour had spread that the school might be performing it at Christmas. Betty had taken her to see the beautiful little theatre in the modern part of the school building, which had its own little foyer, its walls decorated with dancing figures, its own separate entrance from the street and even its own cloakrooms.

Upstairs was the beautifully-equipped theatre itself, with a stage so large that Bernie thought all the dance and theatre companies at home would have been fighting to hire it if it had been in Dublin. Only the fear of being late for character class had prevented her from performing on it there and then for an imaginary audience.

Then, during repertory class that day, the rumour was confirmed. Bernie's eyes shone with excitement. It seemed as if her dream of performing on that splendid stage for a real live audience was about to come true. Then suddenly a terrible thought struck her. There were only five girls in the Arabian Dance. This had been perfect in class, since there were fifteen of them and they had been able to work in three groups, but there wouldn't be three groups in the show.

As Bernie looked around the class her heart sank. There were eight Irish, two Japanese and five Russians. Of course the five Russians would be given the Arabian Dance and, if so, would there by anything at all in the show for the rest of them?

Birthday Offering

Bernie danced the Arabian Dance that morning as she had never danced it before. Not only did she make sure to have every movement correct, but she acted each second of it, pretending to herself that she was dancing in a harem before some great Arab prince and using every twist and turn of her body to make herself attractive to him. But at the end of class the teacher said nothing about who was to dance the piece in the show. Bernie waited anxiously for the next class, but then the Arabian Dance wasn't even mentioned. Instead the teacher announced that today they would learn the battle between the Toy Soldiers and the Mice. When she divided up the class, Sinéad and Shiori were among the Mice and Gráinne, Bernie and Amanda with the Soldiers.

"I don't want to be a stupid soldier," Amanda muttered sulkily, as they got into line. "I want to do the Arabian Dance."

"The Mice and Soldiers are in Act One and the Arabian Dance in Act Two," Gráinne pointed out, "so there's nothing to stop you doing both – if you're good enough!"

As Amanda glared at her, Bernie had to turn away

to hide a smile. Amanda couldn't possibly want to do the Arabian Dance more than she did, but the more she could learn the better. Even being a soldier on a real stage in front of a real live audience would be good. As they began to learn the stiff, jerky movements of the toy soldiers, she thought it was more fun than being a mouse. Not that the casting this time had much to do with talent. It was obvious that the class had been divided according to height, with the smallest picked to be mice. Still, she was glad she was a soldier and even the soldiers had a general. The General would probably be one of the Russians too, but it was something to try for. If Amanda chose to sulk it was her problem.

Sinéad didn't mind being one of the mice. Everything was new and exciting to her. Only eighteen months ago she had been pleading with her mother to let her learn ballet and now here she was preparing for a show. And her new friend was a mouse too. She put up her hands like claws on either side of her face and scurried, mouse-like, after Shiori. But still the class she most looked forward to was character class.

They were learning the Spanish Dance from *The Nutcracker* now and she was again teamed with Misha. Of course only one pair would do it in the show and it was most unlikely to be her, but she was enjoying herself. Misha's flamboyant performance drove her on to try to match him in haughty bearing and fiery gestures. They could talk more easily now that her Russian and his English were improving and, when she tripped and sprawled full-length on the floor, they had a good laugh over it.

While the second group of couples took their turn, he whispered something to Larry, whose fair skin suddenly took on a pinkish shade. He was partnering Shiori and, though his unruly mop of sandy hair hardly looked Spanish, he was throwing himself into the dance with athletic enthusiasm. Shiori too seemed to be enjoying herself, Sinéad noticed. When the class ended she changed out of her character shoes and looked around for Shiori, just in time to see her disappearing out the door with Larry. Gráinne was, as usual, talking to Ivan. Hurrying after Shiori and Larry, she caught up with them in the lobby.

"Will you run over our Russian with me before the tea?" she asked Shiori, as she followed her into the street.

"Velly solly, but plomised Lally I help him with shopping," Shiori apologised, as she set off down the street with him in the direction of the Opera House.

"Is that what they're calling it now?" said a sarcastic voice in the doorway behind her. "He might at least have picked a girl who could pronounce his name!"

Turning, Sinéad saw it was Willie.

"I can't think what shopping she could be helping Larry with," she told him. "Larry never has any money and there's nothing much in the shops anyway."

"You'd better 'tly asking Lally' when he gets back," Willie said mockingly.

He sounded more than a bit annoyed, Sinéad thought, but it did seem a little odd that Larry hadn't talked about his shopping plans to Willie. Misha overtook them as they went across to the hostel and they climbed the stairs together. Outside Barbara and Amanda's room they passed Amanda in conversation with Michael.

"Rudi might know," Michael was saying as the others reached the landing and then, on seeing Misha, "Hey! Is there anywhere in this dump that you can get a decent meal?:"

"Is restaurant in town," Misha told him. "Rudi know it."

"He can take us so," Michael said, going on up the next flight of stairs towards his room, turning to call back over the banisters to Amanda, "We can fix the details at tea."

"So Michael's eating in restaurants now, is he?" Willie commented. "No wonder he's too grand to mix with the likes of us."

"As it happens, I'm treating him," Amanda said crushingly. "I got money from home and I'm taking Barbara and the lads for a meal."

"Sorry I spoke," Willie grinned, winking at Sinéad as she turned into her own room.

She got out her Russian notes and started going through them on her own. First Gráinne, then Shiori, she thought. Was she never to have a friend without losing them to some boy? But when Shiori slipped into the seat beside her in the canteen she felt ashamed of herself.

"Is Willie's birthday day after tomollow," she whispered. "Lally tly find him pleasant."

"Did he get something nice?" Sinéad asked, but Shiori shook her head.

"Must tly again tomollow," she said.

In their room that night, Sinéad told Gráinne and Bernie about the birthday.

"I'd like to get him something too," Sinéad said. "Just to make it more like a birthday. I mean, it's miserable having a birthday when you're away and I like Willie."

"So do I," Bernie said. "He makes me laugh. D'you remember him in Malahide at the summer school?"

"Will I ever forget!" Gráinne laughed. "He joined in every single class, including the Master Class, though he'd never done ballet in his life before!"

"You have to admit he's guts," Bernie pointed out. "Maybe we could get him something between us if we could find anything."

"In Cork you could get some little thing in a joke shop if you were stuck," Gráinne said, "but I don't know if we'd even find a birthday card here."

Next morning, however, they had a stroke of luck. Gráinne got a food parcel. When Sinéad saw the huge slab of cherry cake and the apple pie and all the little angel cakes and biscuits her Aunt Nan used to bake when she stayed with them in Cork, her face lit up.

"Just the smell makes me feel I'm in Montenotte," she said. "Look, she's even put in some of those ginger snaps I like so much."

"But don't you see," Gráinne cried, "this solves the problem of Willie's birthday. We can pool any money we can spare and buy Coke and bread and sausage and stuff and have a birthday party!"

Larry was delighted with the suggestion, having almost given up hope of finding a suitable present that he could afford. So, next day after Sinéad finished her piano lesson, she met the others in the lobby.

"Come on," Larry said, "or Willie will appear and

want to know where we're going. He was suspicious enough yesterday."

"Where is he now?" Sinéad asked, as they hurried away.

"He have piano lesson," Misha told her, "but over now so must hurry."

Willie would certainly have wondered if he had seen them setting off together. Gráinne, Ivan, Bernie and Shiori were with them and, thanks to Ivan and Misha, they had no trouble buying everything they needed.

"Where are we going to put all this stuff so Willie doesn't see it?" Larry asked.

"In our room of course," Gráinne said, "with the stuff I got from home. We'll have the party there anyway. Say nothing to Willie and let on no one knows it's his birthday. Then make an excuse to bring him down to our room after tea."

"Can Shiori ask Fukuyo?" Sinéad asked. "It's awkward sharing a room with someone and not asking them."

"Of course," Gráinne said. "Ivan's asking Max. That makes five boys and five girls. It's perfect."

"I suppose we oughta be able to seat ten between the beds and the chair," Bernie said doubtfully.

"We'll have to use your bed as a table for the food," Gráinne told her, "but it's not a dinner party, for crying out loud. People can sit on the floor or eat standing up. Larry, would you ever go and find Willie and keep him out of the way, so he doesn't see us bring the stuff in?"

Larry found Willie in their room. He expected to be asked where he'd been. Instead he was hardly in the door before Willie shouted at him excitedly.

"Have you heard the news?"

"What?"

"We're starting duet class tomorrow!"

"All of us?"

"Just you and me and Michael. They don't usually start people on duet class their first term, but they're short of boys, so we'll be partnering girls out of the pre-graduation classes."

"Wow!" Larry gasped. "We'll be doing lifts! Let's hope I don't drop anyone!?

"Not a fear of you," Willie laughed. "I'm the one who should worry. Haven't you done weight-lifting and all? And these Russian girls are all so thin if they turned sideways they'd be marked absent!"

"It's not their weight I'm bothered about," Larry told him. "It's getting them properly balanced."

"Isn't that what we'll be getting taught?" Willie pointed out. "I can't wait to start. It's the best present I could have . . . I mean, the best thing that could happen."

Larry pretended not to notice the slip. It was going to be hard enough pretending he didn't know about the birthday until evening, though with post so uncertain there might well be nothing special to mark the event until the party. The news of the duet class had stopped Willie noticing anything unusual and Larry had no trouble keeping him chattering on about it until the others had had time to store their shopping out of sight.

When the time for the duet class arrived it was even more exciting than they had expected, for they found they each had to lift not just one of the Russian girls but two. Though they had been amazed when they arrived first to find so many boys at a ballet school, there were still only half as many as girls and, as a result, the boys had to do everything twice in order to give all the girls a turn, partnering first one and then the other.

At first Willie kept apologising to his partners, explaining he was new to duet class, but they shook their head, laughing. One in particular, a pretty, dark-haired girl called Elena, with high cheekbones, brown eyes and long black lashes, was really nice about it.

"Niet, niet," she laughed, waving his apologies aside. "Is OK. You careful. Better than Russian boy."

Their teacher, a former member of the State Ballet Company at the Opera House, gave them confidence from the start and they were surprised at how quickly they learned to do simple lifts. Nevertheless, by the end of class they were exhausted, having had to work twice as hard as the girls. Moreover, thin though the girls might be, it took a great deal of energy to lift them again and again. Mopping his brow with a tissue, Willie heard Elena's rippling laugh.

"Ya oostal," he admitted, glad he had learned the day before how to say he was tired in Russian.

She laughed again as she waved goodbye.

"Doh zveedaneeyah," she smiled. "See you next class."

He was lucky to have so friendly a partner, Willie thought. Despite what he had said to Larry, he had had nightmares the previous night about girls screaming at him in Russian for being clumsy. When he told Misha this, he agreed.

"You very lucky," he said. "Elena best one in class. Would be in graduation class only too young. Everyone say Madame have great hope for her. Is strange she work with beginner."

. . . the boys had to do everything twice in order
to give all the girls a turn . . .

But Gráinne, whose Russian was already remarkable, was able to explain.

"Ivan says Elena has been working with Igor," she told him. "He's going to be brilliant, Ivan says, but he's more interested in dancing than partnering. Twice he let Elena slip last week and Madame was worried for her."

In that case, Willie thought, it seemed remarkable that she should entrust her to a beginner, but who was he to question his good fortune? As he let the water from the shower run over his aching muscles, he decided it was another birthday present, to make up for the total absence of cards and parcels from home.

All the same, after a particularly ghastly canteen meal he was a bit depressed. *Kasha* and cucumber salad was hardly his idea of a birthday meal and, by the time Larry stopped him halfway up the stairs to their room and told him Sinéad wanted to see him, his usual good humour had deserted him.

"Can't it wait till tomorrow?" he said impatiently. "I'm tired from duet class."

"She said it was urgent," Larry told him, "and it's on your way."

"What on earth can she want that's urgent?" Willie grumbled, as he crossed the landing and knocked on the door of the girls' room. He heard someone call out, "Come in!" and pushed open the door, to be greeted by a chorus of voices:

"Happy birthday to you,
Happy birthday to you,
Happy birthday, dear Willie,
Happy birthday to you!"

The room was full of people: Irish, Russian and Japanese. Willie stood there, gaping.

"How did you know it was my birthday?" he gasped finally.

"Larry saw it on your passport," Bernie told him. "Come on in and shut the door or we'll have to feed the whole hostel."

It was only then that Willie saw the food. Spread out on the nearest bed was a big sheet of plastic that looked as if it had once covered something returned from the cleaners. Laid out on that were piles of buttered bread, sliced sausage, tomatoes, apples, buns, cakes, biscuits, bags of nuts and crisps, bars of chocolate and an apple pie. And on the table were bottles of Coke and an assortment of toothmugs.

"Yippee!" Willie cried. "Wherever did you get all the goodies?"

"They're a present from all of us," Bernie told him, "especially Gráinne because she got a lot of it from home. Are you right, Gráinne?"

"Right!" came Gráinne's voice from somewhere at the back of the room and the crush of bodies somehow parted to show Gráinne, holding out an upturned tin lid on which was a cake with fourteen lighted candles.

For a moment Willie was speechless.

"A cake!" he breathed, when he had recovered his speech. "Thanks a million! It's deadly!"

"We'd a terrible hunt for candles," Gráinne told him, "but Ivan found them in the end in a shop right the other side of town. Now you have to blow them all out and cut the cake so we can eat it. I'm afraid it's only cherry."

"Cherry's fantastic!" Willie said, taking a deep breath and blowing out all the candles at one go.

As the clapping and cheering died away, Larry turned to Willie.

"I hope you can find room for a bit of cake," he said, "after all that *kasha*!"

Everyone fell about laughing and then fell on the food. Never had cakes, biscuits, apples and Coke seemed so like manna from heaven.

"That's one thing about meals here," Willie said. "You really enjoy real food when you get it."

Certainly between the ten of them they had no trouble polishing off the lot. Then they sang songs and told jokes until Willie got phone calls from his father in Leeds and his mother in Dublin, one after the other. That broke up the party for they all had class first thing in the morning. Then, next day, the first of Willie's birthday presents arrived.

He opened the package with its English stamps in some excitement, since his father had said on the phone that there was something in the post for him. His face fell when he saw the tube of toothpaste. Was someone having him on? Then he remembered he had warned his father in his letter about the mail robberies and he examined the package more carefully. The toothpaste tube was inside its carton, but the toothpaste had been squeezed out. Rolled tight inside it, kept clean within the thin plastic bag banks use for giving out coins, was a fifty dollar note.

So it was a good-humoured bunch which set off for their respective classes that morning, except for Amanda. When she boasted over breakfast about the success of her dinner party the previous evening, she found the wind taken out of her sails.

"I'm so glad you had a nice evening," Gráinne told her sweetly. "I don't feel so guilty about not inviting you to the party."

If that put Amanda's nose out of joint it was nothing to the rage she felt when the cast list for *The Nutcracker* went up on the notice board. Like Gráinne and Bernie, she was listed amongst the Toy Soldiers in Act One, but had nothing in Act Two. Bernie, on the other hand, was listed with four Russian girls to do the Arabian Dance.

"I don't see why Bernie should get to do the Arabian Dance," she complained to Michael. "It's not fair. I bet it's because she's been Madame's little pet ever since she injured her back in Dublin."

"Try saying that to Madame!" grinned Michael.

"Maybe I will so," Amanda scowled.

"Rather you than me," Michael told her. "You'll get blown out of it and she won't change her mind."

"She might have to," Amanda said fiercely. "I might make her!"

"You and who else?" Michael teased. "Forget it, Amanda. There'll be other shows."

But Amanda didn't forget it and Bernie got even more dirty looks. Then one day Bernie was going down the steep flight of stairs at the hostel when the sound of rushing feet behind her made her glance back. Before she could move out of the way, something hit her a blow across the back. Crying out in pain, she stumbled, missed her footing and fell all the way down the stairs to the bottom, her left leg crumpled beneath her.

Duet Class

The sound of Bernie's fall brought people running from nearby rooms.

"Are you all right?" Gráinne cried anxiously, as Bernie tried to pull herself to her feet.

"I think I've done something to my leg," she said, her eyes filling with tears.

"Is the pain real bad?" Sinéad asked sympathetically.

"It's not that," Bernie wept, "but if I've broken something I won't be able to dance in the show."

"What happened?" Willie asked as he reached them. "Did you fall downstairs?"

"No," Bernie sobbed. "Someone pushed me."

"Who do this to you?" Misha demanded, but just then Betty arrived on the scene.

"Never mind that now," she ordered. "Misha, run over to the office and tell them Bernie's hurt her leg. And you, Bernie, sit down and try to relax."

She helped Bernie to a sitting position on the third step and examined the leg.

"Can you straighten it?" she asked.

"Sort of," Bernie said, wincing with pain, "but it hurts."

"I don't think it's broken," Betty said. "More likely

you've sprained it or pulled a muscle or something, but don't try to move it till Anna's had a look at it. Don't worry! People are always injuring themselves here. They'll have you fixed up in no time."

"But not in time to dance in the show," Bernie cried.

"Oh, come on now," Betty soothed. "It's weeks and weeks away yet. Think positive. Are you sure you were pushed?"

Bernie nodded.

"I heard someone come thundering down the stairs behind me," she said, "and then I felt a clatter on my back and down I went."

"Maybe it was an accident," Betty suggested.

"So why didn't whoever it was stick around to pick up the pieces?" Willie asked, "instead of disappearing in a puff of smoke? D'you know who it was, Bernie?"

"I'm not sure," Bernie told him. "It happened so fast."

"But you've a fair idea, haven't you?" Gráinne persisted.

"I didn't see her face," Bernie said reluctantly.

"So at least you know it was a female," Willie said.

"Don't you know it was!" Gráinne retorted. "None of the boys would be likely to be put into the Arabian Dance in her place if she injured herself, would they?"

"Oh, Gráinne!" Sinéad cried. "She wouldn't, would she?"

Before Gráinne could reply, Anna arrived and put a stop to the conversation. Trained in physiotherapy, Anna examined the leg and pronounced it unbroken. Then she told Larry and Willie to help Bernie up the stairs to her room and sent everyone else about their business. As soon as peace had been restored, she set about working on the leg.

"First trouble with this," she smiled, touching Bernie's throat, "now this."

"I'm sorry," Bernie told her tearfully, "but it's not my fault. Someone knocked me down the stairs."

"Accident," Anna said.

Bernie hesitated. She was almost sure it was Amanda and no accident at all, but she knew how her father despised a telltale.

"Never grass on your mates," he had said to her more than once. "No matter what they done. There's never been an informer in our family, an' please God there never will, so don't be running home with tales out of school!"

But this is different, she told herself. If Amanda's let get away with this, the dear knows what she might do next time. And if she got to dance the Arabian Dance instead of me on account of it, wouldn't she deserve to be told on? Worse, I'll bloody kill her! But maybe her father wouldn't think that was worse. The thought of not being able to dance the Arabian Dance made her eyes fill with tears again.

"Pain bad?: Anna asked, as a hot tear fell on her hand.

"I don't mind if you can fix it," Bernie told her between clenched teeth. "I'm only worried how soon I'll be able to dance again?"

"Maybe next week? Week after?" Anna told her, shrugging.

"Will that mean I'll still be able to dance in the show?" Bernie asked eagerly.

"Ah, show! *Da, da*. Leg better for show," Anna laughed.

"Then it doesn't matter how much you hurt!" Bernie cried.

And I won't tell on Amanda either, she thought, because her mean little plot didn't work. But I'll take bloody good care she doesn't get a chance to do it again! And I'll warn all the others in case they ever get between her and it.

Even though she couldn't dance for the next fortnight, Bernie went to all her classes, watching to make sure she missed nothing, while Anna continued working on her leg. She also took all her Russian and piano classes as usual and was delighted to find she was able to play a Russian folk song. Because she loved music so much, she played with feeling as soon as she had mastered the notes and her progress was faster than she had dared to hope. All the same, she knew it would be a long time before she could play like Shiori.

Sometimes she would linger for a minute or two outside the studio while Shiori was practising, wishing that she too could play the Chopin Waltz in G Flat, to which she had once danced on Dún Laoghaire pier.

"One day I'll play it," she vowed, as she limped off down the passage.

Sitting watching character class she noticed how two of the couples in the Spanish Dance seemed to have become couples outside class also. Through his friendship with Shiori, Larry seemed more and more often to be in a group with Sinéad and Misha, so that even though he and Willie were still pals, anything requiring even numbers tended to leave Willie odd man out.

Bernie herself still missed having Eileen to confide in,

but was far more concerned about how soon she would be able to dance again than about her lack of a special friend, especially as she got on well with nearly everyone. Willie, on the other hand, was clearly put out. His usual bouncy good spirits seemed to have disappeared and the others no longer forgot the poor food as they laughed at the comic things he said about it. He complained a good deal of the cold and his temper seemed to shorten with the days, as it grew dark earlier and earlier. Then one morning he was awakened by something cold and wet on his face and the sound of Larry's laughter.

How dare Larry play the old wet sponge trick on him, he thought. Then he realised the room was unusually bright. Had he overslept? He glanced anxiously at the alarm clock. But it was still ticking away, the small band at the seven. The sun could never be up yet. Why was it so bright?

Then he saw the thick white line along the window sill. Snow! With a yell he leaped out of bed, grabbed a handful, moulded it into a ball and flung it at Larry. But Larry was ready with another and returned fire with interest. Misha, used to snow for five or six months of every year, watched them with an indulgent smile, like a father watching children at play, till one of Willie's snowballs caught him on the ear. Then, still in his pyjamas like the others, he joined in and the pitched three-way battle only ended, amidst laughter, when there was no snow left on the window ledge. Collapsing on his bed, Willie looked at the little patches of wet snow, melting on the floor, and shook his head.

"We'd better get this mopped up before anyone sees

it," he said, "and we'd better hurry up about it or we'll be late."

Using tights from the little pile waiting to be washed, they soaked up the worst of the melted snow, dressed and ran out on to the street. All around them snow was spread like a white coverlet over roadway and pavement, except for the footprints crossing between hostel and school, which soon became a dirty, slushy brown pathway.

"It's not so cold now," Willie exclaimed in surprise.

"Always warmer when snow come," Misha told him. "Will be colder soon."

Willie turned to ask Larry if he had an extra sweater in his case for the really cold weather, but he had disappeared. Turning he saw him swinging Shiori high above a big drift of snow and threatening to drop her into it. As Shiori's squeals mingled with Larry's laughter Willie turned away in disgust.

It didn't help, he thought, that he was only a Mouse in the end-of-term *Nutcracker*. Admittedly Larry was also a Mouse, but then Shiori was too and that helped to console Larry. Willie knew it was unreasonable to expect to have a partnering role when he was still in his first term at duet class. All the same, he looked enviously at the boys in graduation class, especially Rudi, who was dancing the Prince. Of course that was the lead, a role for which any boy might aim, for he would be partnering Nadia, already tipped for entry in next year's International Ballet Congress in Moscow. But it was not the great *pas de deux* with the Sugar Plum Fairy in the final act that Willie was thinking of as much as the moments when he would lift Clara, for Clara would be Elena and she was *his* partner.

"I wish I had a real dancing role in *Nutcracker*," he said to her, as they warmed up for that afternoon's duet class. "If only I had done duet class in Ireland before I came, but there weren't enough boys at Miss Byrne's to do it. And I'm not good at character dance like Misha," for Misha and Sinéad had, to everyone's astonishment, been listed to do the Spanish Dance.

"Character, no," Elena replied, shaking her head. "Character is also not for me. I dream one day I dance *Giselle*. Maybe have you for partner."

"But I could never dance Albrecht," Willie admitted ruefully. "My feet are not good enough."

"But you good partner," Elena told him. "With you I feel safe. One day I hope we dance on stage together."

Suddenly Willie felt good. Maybe now he was only a Mouse, but Elena wanted him for a partner. His partnering was particularly good in class that day, as his teacher told him afterwards. The remains of his fifty dollars burned his hand when he automatically checked it was still safely hidden as he pulled on his sweater.

"Would you like to come down to the Dragon Café for a bun after tea this evening?" he asked Elena suddenly, his heart in his mouth.

There was a pause, which seemed to Willie to go on for ages. Then Elena smiled.

"*Da,*" she said. "I like very much."

Willie took the stairs to the shower two at a time and Larry, showering next door, heard his voice rise easily over the double downpour in a chorus of "Any Dream Will Do." Moreover, during tea in the canteen he remarked to Sinéad and Misha that the mashed potato was so watery the meal should be called "Sausage and

Splash." It was clear that he was back to his old form.

After a few weeks Bernie was doing class again but now Amanda's sour looks were returned with interest. While Bernie had been watching class, Amanda had made a big effort. She had managed to lose weight and had put her heart into her dancing so she had frequently won a word or two of praise from the teacher, but now it was clear that Bernie would be able to do the Arabian Dance after all, she seemed to lose heart once more.

"She'd want to watch it," Gráinne said after class one day, "or Madame won't want her back next year. She's no sympathy with anyone who gets fat."

"She's been at the chocolates again," Sinéad told them. "She's got a terrible sweet tooth. I don't know how she managed to lose weight so fast while Bernie was out of action."

"I do," Bernie told her. "Did you not notice how she had to keep running to the toilet? She took tablets to make her go."

"Would that make you lose weight?" Sinéad asked.

"It would, but it's very bad for you," Gráinne told her, "so don't you ever try it."

"I can't see Sinéad ever needing to," Bernie said. "No matter what she eats, she never seems to get any fatter, the lucky thing. I wish I was like that. I've been dying for something sweet ever since I got here and I've only to look at a chocolate box to get fat. If Mammy kept sending me cakes and chocolates the way Amanda's mother does I know I'd end up stuffing myself too."

"You would not, because you'd share them with your friends," Gráinne pointed out. "Amanda's too selfish to do that. And she's greedy. Wouldn't you think her mother would have more sense than to keep sending her chocolate and she a dance teacher? I mean, she oughta know dancers have to stay slim."

"Maybe she thinks Amanda has one or two a day," Bernie said, "but it's awful hard to do that with chocolate. And anyways Amanda's not only getting fat. She's lazy. She only worked really hard when she thought she might get my part."

"And she wouldn't have," Sinéad said. "I bet Natasha would have got it, or Gráinne."

"If they hadn't both been bumped into by accident on purpose on an icy bit of street," Bernie said grimly. "It could have been like one of them who-dunnits, where everyone with a claim to the money except the murderer gets killed one by one!"

"We'd better all watch out for her now," Sinéad agreed, "because it would be real easy for her to make someone slip and injure themselves with the streets the way they are now."

Indeed, they had all slipped at least once without anyone pushing them, for the streets and pavements had suddenly become like glass. The lovely soft snow of the early falls had been ground down, layer upon layer, under their feet and frozen over. Ploughs cleared the roads each morning for traffic, pushing the snow into great banks on either side. Then the weak midday sun would be just sufficient to thaw the top layer into a trickle of water which covered the pavement with a thin film, later freezing into a thin sheet of ice.

Sliding and clutching at each other amidst giggles, it gave Gráinne a great excuse to hang on to Ivan's arm, for the Russians seemed to have no trouble keeping their footing. After a few weeks, however, the Irish too learned how to walk safely on the slippery paths.

"It's only great for the leg muscles," Larry told Shiori. "Walking day after day on ice is better than dancing and athletics put together for developing control."

They were on their way back to the hostel from a Sunday afternoon performance in the Opera House. A whole group of them had gone to see the ballet company in a Russian rock musical about Orpheus and Eurydice. Much improved though their Russian was by now, it was still not so good that they could follow all the dialogue, spoken or sung, but then even Elena seemed unable to follow it all.

"He say to her to go with him," she explained to Willie.

"I gathered that much," Willie said, "but why did the other guy chase everyone away?"

Elena shook her head, laughing.

"Is not same like in Greek story," was all she could manage by way of reply, "but he is very fine dancer." -

"Tell me about it," Willie agreed. "If I could do a series of *grand jetés* like that I'd die happy."

"But why die?" Elena laughed. "Then you make *premier danseur*!"

"Instead of a miserable mouse," Willie said. "I'm getting bored running round the stage and twiddling my whiskers."

"Mouse is better than what I do in my first show," Elena told him. "I small doll in workshop of Dr Coppelius who sit all act without movement until Swanhilda wind me. Then all I do is nod head!"

"I guess we all have to start small," Willie agreed. "Maybe next year I'll have something more exciting to do."

"Maybe next term when parents come," Elena told him. "They come for Irish Easter. Is different time from Russian Easter."

"Like Christmas," Willie nodded. "It's going to seem awful strange not going home for Christmas."

"You get holiday for Russian Christmas," Elena shrugged. "Is not long after. Then you back only eight, nine weeks your Mama come see you dance."

"I doubt it," Willie said. "She's a doctor. She'd never be able to get away for long enough."

"Tell her take holiday," Elena told him. "Even doctor need holiday."

"I'll talk to her about it over Christmas," Willie said. "I mean, when I get home."

Like Willie, the rest of the Irish students all felt a little odd about not going home for Christmas.

"And I haven't even bought Mam a Christmas present yet," Sinéad said.

"What's the point?" Gráinne argued. "You can't get anything decent here and heaven knows would the parcel ever arrive. Betty says the thing to do is to shop in Moscow on the way back. We'll have a morning there and she says you can get vodka and caviar fairly cheap if you know where to go. Dad ought to be very happy with that."

"You could get vodka in the shop belonging to the Dragon Café," Sinéad pointed out.

"And have to lug it on and off the train," Gráinne told her. "Much better buy it in Moscow, and maybe get it cheaper there. And Betty says the street markets have loads of little souvenirs like those Russian dolls that fit one inside the other, getting smaller and smaller."

"I can't get one of those for Niall," Sinéad pointed out. "I don't know what I could get for him here."

"Why don't you ask Misha what to get him?" Gráinne suggested.

"I wish he was coming to Moscow with us," Sinéad said, "but his home's in the opposite direction in Ekaterinburg."

They were changing for the first dress rehearsal of the show and there was a feeling of tension in the air. They had been working on the fight between the mice and the toy soldiers for so long that they knew exactly what they had to do, but there was a sense of expectation about working on stage in costume and with stage lighting. Sinéad was looking forward to the second act, when she and Misha could strike sparks off each other in the Spanish Dance, but there was such a feeling of strained nerves coming from the corner beside her where Bernie was getting made up that she began to feel anxious herself.

As Bernie painted the toy soldier's red circles on her cheeks, she could think of nothing but the fact that Madame Chumakova would be out front, her black eyes following every movement on stage. She, Bernie, alone of all the first-year Irish students had been trusted with a dancing role in the classical repertoire. It was her chance to prove that the money her mother had borrowed at such high interest had not been wasted. Standing beside Gráinne in the wings, waiting to march on stage, she had to wrench her mind back from Act

Two, forcing herself to concentrate on the things that must be done first.

The battle scene took place without any problems but, as Bernie changed out of her red and white tunic and navy trousers into green silky harem pants for the Arabian Dance, she found her hands were trembling so much she had difficulty undoing the fastening of her tunic. She was still shaking with nerves as she joined the other four girls in the wings.

As the opening bars of their dance began her body instinctively responded to the discipline of the repeated rehearsals and the seductive music. As they finished, a sense of relief flooded over her. It was all going to work. She would be able to do it. She crept into a corner of the wings to watch the *Pas de Deux*, dreaming that one day she would dance the Sugar Plum Fairy, glittering in silver and white, as delicate and precise as the tinkling Tchaikovsky score. Suddenly she heard her name.

"But where is Bernadette?"

The angry shout brought her back to reality with a sickening jolt. Lost in her dreams, she had missed her re-entrance for the line-up of all the second act cast for the finale. Crimson in the face, she ran into her place.

"Why you not enter at right time?" screamed Madame Chumakova from the front row of the circle.

"I'm sorry, Madame. I was dreaming," Bernie stammered.

"You dream in bed, not in theatre," Madame raged. "This is not play for children."

"No, Madame. I'm very sorry, Madame!" Bernie gasped, but Madame Chumakova was still not satisfied.

As they finished, a sense of relief flooded over her.

"I make you more sorry," she roared. "You miss entrance one more time I send you home to Mama!"

The whole school seemed to be staring at Bernie and there was nowhere to hide. As soon as they had rehearsed the finale and curtain calls she fled into the darkest corner of the scene dock, the tears streaking her face with mascara. All the work and effort she had put into getting and keeping her role had been for nothing. With a few seconds loss of concentration she had thrown it all away.

Pas de Deux

"Poor Bernie," Sinéad said in the dressing-room. "I felt so sorry for her, with everyone looking at her. Madame wouldn't really send her home, would she?"

"She only said she would if it ever happened again," Gráinne pointed out, "and you can be dead sure it won't! Not after that! No matter what Bernie does for the rest of her life you can bet she'll never again let her mind wander coming up to an entrance."

"All the same," Amanda smirked, "it was very unprofessional of her. Getting a role like that and not minding what she was at! She doesn't deserve to be left in it, if you ask me!"

"I *didn't* ask you," Gráinne snapped, "and Madame might do more than shout if she thought someone had tried to injure one of her students."

"I don't know what you're talking about," Amanda sniffed, tossing her head, but she turned away and buried herself in removing cream.

Just then Elena stuck her head in the door. She had already changed out of her Clara costume and taken off her make-up.

"Hi, Elena!" Gráinne said. "You were deadly!"

"Was OK?" Elena asked anxiously.

"More than OK," Gráinne told her. "I'd be thrilled skinny if I was half as good as you."

"But I student here since nine-years-old," Elena said. "I should be more good."

"Better," Gráinne corrected her. "In English you say 'better,' not 'more good.' But it's not true anyway. You couldn't have been better than you were today."

"Thank you," Elena said. "But where is Bernie?"

"She never came back to change," Sinéad said. "I hope she's OK. I mean, she looked desperate upset."

"I go find," Elena told her.

Sobbing in the scene dock, Bernie suddenly felt an arm around her shoulders and stiffened.

"Not cry!" Elena whispered. "Is nothing."

"Nothing?" Bernie cried. "I've only blown it all! Wrecked my chances, big-time!"

Elena shook her head, laughing.

"Madame only shout to frighten you, because you good dancer," she said. "If Amanda do such a thing, she say, 'Let fat pig stay in wings. Tomorrow Natasha do it'!"

"What?" Bernie turned a tear-stained face to Elena in alarm.

"Today she not say this," Elena told her. "You do Arabian Dance tomorrow, so is nothing!"

"Are you sure she won't replace me?" Bernie asked anxiously.

"Madame say always what she mean," Elena assured her. "She want cast change she say it now. I tell to you, Bernie, always she shout when she think you make good dancer. She think is important you learn lesson."

"Did she ever shout at you?" Bernie asked, scrubbing at her eyes with a tissue.

Elena pulled a face.

"All time she shout at me," she said, "but always I remember what Katerina tell me."

"You mean the ould one in charge of the cloakrooms?"

Elena now had Bernie's full attention and her words were no longer half-smothered in sobs.

"She remember when Pavlova was student here," she nodded. "She say Madame always cross with her. Shout all time: 'This not right! That bad! You try harder!' Pavlova is all time crying. Now she big star in Bolshoi."

"You mean, when Madame thinks someone has talent she keeps on at them all the time to make them even better?" Bernie asked slowly.

Elena nodded again.

"Katerina say, 'Wait till you in Graduation Class.' Next year I go to this class. Already I have the nightmare, but Katerina say must be strong. Is no good for dancer if not strong. You also, Bernie."

"Oh, I'll be strong," Bernie cried. "I don't care how much she shouts at me if it means she thinks I'm worth taking trouble over. And I'll never, never, never miss an entrance again."

"This I believe," Elena laughed. "Someone have to tie you down, stop you going on stage!"

Bernie jumped to her feet.

"I must get changed," she said. "Thanks, Elena. I was feeling desperate. Only for what you said I'd never have been able to face the others."

"Is important only you dance good in show," Elena told her. "Remember this."

On the day of the show it was snowing hard. Looking out of the window first thing Bernie saw that all the footprints had been covered over and, no sooner had the snowplough cleared the roadway, than a thin white sheet spread over it once more.

"I hope the snow doesn't keep the audience away," she said, but Gráinne only laughed.

"They don't even notice the snow here, they're so used to it," she said. "They'll just bring dry shoes in a bag, the way they do to the Opera House."

"Only we don't have three huge cloakrooms with attendants to look after all the wet boots and coats," Sinéad pointed out.

"And we don't have three tiers of seating either," Gráinne told her. "The cloakroom off the foyer's big enough for the number of people we can seat and they'll probably lay on cloakroom attendants too."

"Maybe Katerina will take charge," Bernie said, thinking of the hundreds of shows she must have seen in the fifty years she had been there.

Since Elena had told her about Katerina's advice, she had made a point of chatting to the old lady and found she knew boys and girls who had become soloists in the ballet company of every state capital of the former Soviet Union.

"I do wish Mam could be here to see the show," Sinéad said. "She was so glad I was learning the Spanish Dance. She said in her last letter that there have always been close links between the cultures of Ireland and Spain."

"She'd still rather you did folk dancing than ballet then," Bernie suggested.

"Oh, not any more," Sinéad told her. "She's happy enough about me doing ballet since the Minister told her it was important for the Irish to make their mark in the world of ballet too."

"Is that what we're supposed to be doing?" Gráinne giggled. "You could have fooled me!"

"Did you tell her you're doing the Spanish Dance in the show?" Bernie asked.

"I wrote her the minute I knew," Sinéad said, "but she never answered. I haven't had a letter from her for weeks now. I thought she'd be so pleased about it that she'd write by return."

"You know how funny the post is," Bernie reminded her.

"But I got a letter from Niall," Sinéad argued, "and he *never* writes."

"At least you got all the news from home," Bernie pointed out, but Sinéad shook her head.

"He wrote about school and that it had rained for days and there'd been a bus strike. He never said if Mam got my letter. Just that she and Dad sent their love."

"She's probably busy with Irish classes and everything, coming up to the Christmas," Gráinne shrugged.

That morning there was still no letter for Sinéad, but there was one for Gráinne.

"Does Aunt Nan say anything about Mam?" Sinéad asked, but Gráinne shook her head.

"It's all about making the Christmas pudding and how she was baking cakes for the old Folks' Party and rubbish like that," she said.

But later, when they were leaving the boots and coats in the school cloakroom, Gráinne held Bernie back as Sinéad hurried out after Misha and Larry.

"There *was* something in my letter about Aunt Phil," she said. "She's had a heart attack and she's in the Mater Hospital."

"That's desperate!" Bernie cried. "Why ever didn't you tell Sinéad?"

"Aunt Phil didn't want her upset," Gráinne said, "when she was so far away and everything."

"But she'll have to know in the end," Bernie said. "I mean, her mother could be still in hospital when we go home."

"Oh, she will be," Gráinne told her. "She has to have a bypass operation. Otherwise they wouldn't be keeping her in over the Christmas."

"I keep forgetting it's nearly Christmas at home now," Bernie said. "But you can't leave Sinéad to get home not knowing!"

"That's why Aunt Phil asked Mammy to write and tell me," Gráinne explained. "So I can tell Sinéad before she gets back. But she doesn't want her to know till the last minute, because she'd only worry all the time when there's nothing she can do. And maybe by the time we're going home the operation will be over and Aunt Phil on the mend."

"But you're not going to stop Sinéad worrying by not telling her," Bernie argued. "She expected her mother to 'phone on Sunday and she smelled a rat when she got Niall's letter."

"Maybe Aunt Phil will be well enough to write herself soon," Gráinne told her. "I mean, they have to get her better before she's fit for the operation and if anything awful happened they'd ring."

"Janey!" Bernie gasped. "Poor Sinéad! Would it not have been better to say your mother had been talking to hers on the 'phone?"

"Then she'd have asked to see the letter," Gráinne said. "And if I've got to tell her the truth before we get back the fewer lies I have to tell now the better. I just want to try to take her mind off home. Will you help me?"

"Of course, if I can," Bernie told her but, sorry though she was for Sinéad, she was determined that nothing would distract her from the show.

All the same, she didn't forget to stick her head into the next-door dressing-room and wish Elena good luck. Elena was twiddling the ends of the ringlets she wore as Clara and Bernie suddenly realised she was as nervous as herself. Then she wondered why she was surprised. Elena might be brilliant but Clara was a very important role. Wasn't the nutcracker *her* Christmas present and the whole rest of the ballet *her* dream?

"You haven't a thing to worry about," Bernie told her. "You'll be deadly, like you always are. I just came to say good luck."

"And I wish you good luck also," Elena smiled, smoothing the folds of Clara's blue party dress as Bernie hurried away.

Watching the opening from the wings as the Mice waited for their entrance, Sinéad thought Elena was almost as good as the soloist that she and Shiori had seen in the Opera House.

"And she's not much taller than us either," she

whispered to Shiori. "Maybe next time the school does *Nutcracker* we could do Clara."

"Must each do one performance," Shiori giggled, "otherwise we deadly livals! Then I push you downstairs to get part!"

"Sh!" Larry hissed. "If they hear you chattering they'll run the lot of us and we won't be let back until after the party scene."

"And Elena will freak out," Willie said. "She's up to high doh already. She's deadly, isn't she? Next year she'll be in the graduation class."

"And looking for a new partner," Larry teased.

"No, she won't!" Willie said indignantly. "She said it won't make any difference. We can still work together."

"Sh!" Max ordered, as he joined them.

In the presence of the older boy, dancing the small soloist role of Leader of the Mice, they all fell silent. Watching Elena's Clara, being comforted by her mother over her broken toy, Sinéad suddenly thought again of her own mother. Maybe wearing her hair scraped back off her face in a bun did give her rather a severe look and maybe she was impatient with people who didn't put the Irish language and Irish dancing before everything else, but she had always been there for Sinéad whenever she had been hurt or upset.

Then, as the last of the stage mothers rounded up their children and Clara was sent to bed, the lights changed, the Christmas tree grew taller and taller and the Mice lined up in the wings for their entrance, no longer thinking of anything except their cue. As usual, the time they were on stage seemed to pass in a flash and then they were back in the dressing-room, changing for Act Two.

. . . the Mice lined up in the wings for their entrance . . .

"How d'you think it went?" Sinéad asked Gráinne.

"OK," Gráinne said. "I heard a few laughs during the fight."

"Is that good?" Sinéad asked doubtfully.

"Of course," Gráinne told her. "Don't you think toy soldiers firing cannon at mice is meant to be funny?"

"But I thought we were the baddies," Sinéad said.

"Comic baddies. Hey, listen!"

From the distant auditorium they heard applause as the curtain came down at the end of Act One.

"They're still clapping," Bernie said. "They must like it so. Let's hope they like the second act as much."

As she pulled on her Spanish dress with all the layers and ruffles, Sinéad seemed to change. Even sitting in front of the mirror she looked haughty as she tossed her hair back off her head before fastening it up with curved combs. And, as she fixed the gold rings to her ears her big eyes flashed. She was no longer the youngest Irish student, eager to please, but a temperamental Spanish beauty, proud and fiery.

There was a tap on the door and Misha stuck his head cautiously around it.

"We go now?" he asked.

"Wait a minute," Sinéad ordered.

She reddened her lips, turned this way and that, examining herself in detail, and then flounced to his side. Misha grinned.

"You like real gypsy girl," he said as they made their way towards the stage.

Gráinne looked after them in amusement.

"My little cousin's growing up," she commented. "Well, at least she's not worrying about Aunt Phil now!"

Listening to the buzz of conversation on the other side of the curtain as the audience returned to its seats after the interval, Sinéad felt her heart pounding. Only eighteen months after she had taken her first secret ballet class at the Dance Congress in Malahide, she was about to go on stage before a Russian audience with a handsome Russian partner. It didn't seem possible.

"Pinch me!" she whispered to Misha, as the curtain rose on the second act.

"What you want?" he asked, puzzled.

"Like this," she said, gently squeezing the flesh on his lower arm between her finger and thumb.

He looked bewildered.

"Is for good luck in Ireland?" he suggested.

Sinéad shook her head, laughing.

"To make sure I'm not dreaming," she explained. "Perhaps when you pinch me I'll wake up!"

"I see you don't dream when you dance with me," Misha told her, giving her a pinch on the cheek.

"Ow!" squeaked Sinéad. "Not so hard!"

"Now you awake," Misha grinned. "Now you keep mind on dance."

"Of course," Sinéad told him indignantly. "It's just that I can't believe this is really happening to me."

"When music start you believe," Misha said. "In Russia we wish good luck with kiss."

And quickly he stooped and kissed her. Whether it was the pinch or the kiss that brought the blood to her cheek, Sinéad felt it burn as she heard their music cue. Then everything else was forgotten as she flung herself into their dance.

Holding the final pose, she heard a ripple of

applause and, as they turned to face the audience and she bent in a curtsey, it increased. Bursting with happiness she felt Misha's arm around her waist as he led her downstage for a second curtsey before running with her offstage.

"Up the Dubs!" Bernie whispered to her in the wings, patting her on the back before positioning herself for the Arabian Dance.

That too got a round of applause and Bernie stood back out of the way in the wings until it was time to go on for the finale. Nothing was going to take her mind off her cue this time. Then suddenly she felt a hand on her arm.

"It looked great, Bernie," Sinéad whispered.

"Yours too," Bernie told her. "Another minute and yous both woulda burst into flame!"

Even under her make-up Sinéad blushed.

"Isn't it deadly?" she gasped. "I *do* wish Mam could have been here to see it. I'm only dying to tell her all about it, though telling's not the same as seeing. I don't know why but I keep thinking of her. If I don't get a letter or a 'phone call by Sunday I'm going to 'phone her myself!"

The Sleeping Beauty

"What are we gonna do?" Bernie asked Gráinne that evening, while Sinéad was out of the room. "We can't stop her ringing home if she wants to."

"Maybe I can talk her out of it," Gráinne said. "Can't I say it's hardly worth it when she'll be home soon?"

"I doubt that'll stop her," Bernie told her. "I mean, she's . . ." but she had to break off suddenly as Sinéad appeared in the doorway.

With the excitement of the show behind them they were all thinking about going home now. All the same, the Irish decided they couldn't let the 25th December go by as if it were an ordinary Sunday, just because the Russians didn't think it was Christmas.

"At least we can have a party," Willie said, "and this time we'll have it in *our* room."

Most of them had been sent a few goodies until they could have their real presents when they got home, and it seemed more fun to pool these and have a party. Even Sinéad had got a Christmas cake.

"You see, Aunt Phil didn't forget you," Gráinne pointed out. "She's just been up to her eyes getting ready for the Christmas."

"Maybe that's why she got Niall to wrap the cake for her," Sinéad agreed.

"How d'ya know he did?" Bernie asked.

"'Cos it's his writing on the label," Sinéad told her. "Mam wrote the card all right, but Niall did the rest. And if Mam had wrapped it herself the corners of the paper would have been tucked in. She'd never just have cellophaned it up without folding the corners first."

"I dunno why you wanna be a dancer," Bernie said. "You'd earn much more as a detective."

"I can take the cake to the party now," Sinéad commented, ignoring Bernie's slagging. "Misha was worried he'd nothing he could put towards it, so I wanted something big enough to be from the two of us."

"No one expects the Russians to take anything," Gráinne told her. "Ivan has nothing to bring either but he's not bothered."

"Misha's different from Ivan," Sinéad said. "He's always giving me silly little things. Like last Sunday. We were down on the riverbank and I slipped on a patch of ice and grabbed at this holly tree to stop myself falling. Well, I was nearly buried under all the snow I brought down on top of me. I was trying to get it all brushed off before it melted and drowned me when suddenly there was Misha with this sprig of holly. Somehow the berries must have stayed fresh under all the snow. He gave me a funny little bow and presented it to me like it was a bunch of roses or something."

"You got yourself a right one there," Gráinne teased. "Catch an Irish boy doing anything like that!"

"I think it was lovely of him," Sinéad cried indignantly.

"But then you would, wouldn't you?" Gráinne laughed. "Never mind, you'll grow up one day."

On Sunday morning they were all clustered around the 'phone, willing it to ring. The first call to come through was for Amanda and so eager were they all for even a second-hand contact with Ireland at Christmas that they all crowded round her afterwards.

"Did your mother say anything about the school?" Bernie asked, for whatever she might feel about Amanda, her mother was still principal of the MARIE BYRNE SCHOOL OF DANCE, where her friend Eileen and sister Kylie were still pupils.

"Don't you know they broke up last week?" Amanda sniffed, but at that moment the 'phone rang again and everyone held their breath while Gráinne answered it.

"It's for Larry," Gráinne said, and Larry shouldered his way through the crowd and grabbed the receiver.

"Many happy returns!" he shouted, grinning from ear to ear. ". . . Oh, Mammy, that musta costa fortune! . . . Yes, thanks, I got them OK. Will you be at the airport? . . . Yeah, but Richard says it always takes ages for them to unload the cases so you'd probably make it in time and couldn't they let you off a bit early for once? Things oughta be quiet enough after the Christmas . . . OK, I'll talk to her . . . Hi, Eileen! . . . Same to you!"

Bernie grabbed his arm at the mention of Eileen's name and Larry grinned.

"There's someone here wants a word with you," he said into the mouthpiece and then, to Bernie, "Don't start blathering away like you do at home or Mammy will ate me!"

"Eileen!" Bernie screamed. "Happy Christmas! Howa

113

yeh? . . . Fantastic! I can't wait to see yeh! Will ya come out to the airport? . . . Deadly!"

Then, as Larry tugged at her arm, "OK, OK, I gotta go. 'Bye Eileen! See yah! Here's Larry again."

The calls came through thick and fast after that, with everyone screaming greetings and thanks for parcels and saying, "See you soon!" until only Gráinne and Sinéad were left.

"I'm going down to the post office to ring Mam myself if she doesn't ring soon," Sinéad announced.

"No, hang on a bit," Gráinne told her. "You could be halfway there and a call coming through for you here."

"But she knows it's lunch-time here," Sinéad said. "If she hasn't rung by now she won't ring this morning."

"So maybe she'll ring this evening," Bernie suggested.

"And maybe she won't," Sinéad argued. "I'd rather ring her myself and make sure to catch her before she goes out. I don't mind about missing lunch. It's always disgusting on Sundays."

Gráinne and Bernie both tried to talk her out of it, but Sinéad had made up her mind.

"Will I come with you?" Gráinne asked finally, but Sinéad shook her head.

"I'm not a baby," she said. "I know how to do it and there's no sense in your missing lunch too."

Waiting in the queue for her plate of *kasha* and beetroot, Bernie saw Gráinne's worried look.

"It's no good upsetting yourself," she told her. "Isn't it up to her Da to deal with it when she gets through? Why should you have to tell all the lies for him? Let him tell her the truth or make up his own story."

"I guess you're right," Gráinne agreed. "It's funny, all

the same, that I didn't get a call. It's not like Mammy not to ring and it Christmas."

"Maybe she's having trouble getting through," Bernie suggested. "They let a lot of the operators off over the Christmas. Aren't they always asking people not to make unnecessary calls?"

"So how did all the others get through?" Gráinne asked.

"They were all ringing from Dublin," Bernie pointed out. "Maybe it's worse getting through from Cork."

"I dunno," Gráinne said, "but I hope Uncle Joe tells Sinéad a good story while he's at it."

But when Sinéad got back that afternoon she looked so worried Bernie thought her father must have told her the truth. She was about to say that the operation was nothing these days and she knew scads of people who'd been grand after, when Sinéad's words made her bite her tongue.

"I don't understand it," she said. "The operator kept saying there was no reply. How could they all be out now?"

"Maybe they went to early Mass on account of the Christmas," Bernie suggested.

"But they always get midnight Mass on Christmas Eve," Sinéad said. "I've never known them get eight o'clock on Christmas Day."

"Well they must have today," Gráinne told her. "Look at, there's no point getting worked up over it. Mammy never rang me either, you know."

All the same Sinéad refused to go to the Dragon Café with Misha, Shiori, Larry, Elena and Willie to get coke for the party. She even insisted on leaving the bedroom door open for the rest of the afternoon to be sure of hearing the 'phone, but it never rang. Then, as they were on the landing on the way to the boys' room for the party, there was a call. Betty happened to be in the hall at the time and answered it, calling up the stairs to say it was for Gráinne.

Gráinne took the stairs two at a time and Sinéad followed her, hoping her Aunt Nan could explain the strange silence at home. As she reached the bottom step she heard Gráinne shout:

"Yeah, it's me. Happy Christmas, Mammy! . . . Me too! Howa they all in Cork? . . . Are you? Why so? . . . Oh, I see! . . . Yeah, she's here beside me. . . . OK, but you'll talk to me again afterwards, won't you?"

Turning to Sinéad and holding out the receiver, she said, "Mammy's up staying with Aunt Phil and Aunt Phil wants to talk to you," but before she had finished the sentence, Sinéad had grabbed the receiver.

"Mam?" she cried. "Happy Christmas, Mam! How's Dad and Niall? . . . Oh, it was deadly. I can't wait to tell you all about it . . . What? . . . Oh, yes I got it, thanks. We're going to eat it tonight. It looks fantastic! Where were you all this morning? I tried ringing you . . . What? . . . Are you OK, Mam? You sound awful tired. Were you giving classes right up to Christmas? . . . Oh, OK. . . Yeah, see you soon, Mam . . . Happy Christmas, Aunt Nan. I'll put Gráinne back on to you."

Watching Sinéad chattering away to Shiori and Misha at the party afterwards, Bernie turned to Gráinne.

"She looks happy enough now," she said. "Does that call mean they've let her mother home?"

"Oh no," Gráinne told her. "Mammy and Daddy are

up in Dublin staying with Uncle Joe and Niall over the Christmas so Mammy can cook for them and so they can be near Aunt Phil. That's why they went to a different Mass. Everything's changed to suit hospital visiting hours. While they were in with Aunt Phil Mammy put through the call from the hospital and Aunt Phil was able to talk for a few minutes."

"When's the op?" Bernie asked.

"Soon as she's strong enough," Gráinne said. "Maybe the week after next."

"Janey!" Bernie exclaimed. "Just as we're going home. Sinéad's gonna get an awful shock."

"Tell me about it!" Gráinne said. "Amn't I gonna have to tell her?"

Already the school was awash with rumours about the following term. It was said that Madame intended to do the last act of *The Sleeping Beauty* in the National Concert Hall when they went back to Dublin at the end of their first year so next term they would be working on that.

"Don't you wish you could do Aurora?" Willie asked Elena.

"If I have wish it is to do Blue Bird *Pas de Deux*," she told him. "But what is good of wishing? Is too soon for me. If lucky maybe I get small solo like Cinderella. Maybe have you for my Prince."

"What a hope!" Willie groaned. "From Mouse to Prince in one term! I'll be dead lucky if I'm one of the courtiers."

"We see," Elena smiled. "We both work hard and we see."

The same sort of talk was going on all over the school.

"There's not a lot in it for us," Bernie said gloomily to Betty over lunch, but Betty only laughed.

"Isn't there always the Garland Dance?" she said, "and there'll be loads of other things in the programme as well. Don't you know all the Irish will have to get something if we're taking it to Dublin."

"I wish we could have taken *Nutcracker*," Bernie said. "I'd like Eileen and Mammy to see me in the Arabian Dance, though I'd rather do the girl in the middle."

"And I'd rather be a ballerina with the Kirov!" Betty grinned. "You're always in such a hurry, Bernie. And we don't know for sure what we're taking yet."

All the same, Bernie told herself, they might be thinking about the casting already. It would be wise not to relax just because the show was over and they were going home soon. She redoubled her efforts, not bothering about things like washing clothes. Wouldn't Mammy do them when she got home, and dirty tights and leotards could be rolled up and jammed into the case any old way.

Then, on the day of their final class, Madame suddenly appeared. Bernie never saw her come in but, as she finished a series of turns, she had the prickly sensation of being watched and, looking across to the far end of the mirror, found two black eyes fixed on her.

"You!" Madame shouted, her finger jabbing the air in Bernie's direction. "You! Do it again and this time you finish it!"

"Me?" Bernie stammered. "By myself?"

"*Da*! Stupid girl! Quick!"

Knowing the whole class was looking at her, Bernie

re-positioned herself. What did Madame want her to do that she hadn't done before? She had ended up facing the mirror in the correct position. There was a fluttering in her stomach as if she were about to appear on stage before an audience. As the music began again, she went through the sequence of steps once more.

"Arms!" screamed Madame on the *jetés* and then, as she finished, there was an ominous silence.

"Again!"

Madame bit out the word that seemed to echo round the studio. Everyone stood as if frozen. Her heart pounding, Bernie got control of her trembling limbs and crossed the studio once more. It was like a nightmare. Would it never end?

This time she made sure her arms were fully extended on the *jetés* and that she not only finished neatly, facing the mirror, but that her head was lifted, her eyes looking straight ahead. Surely she was right this time?

"Again!"

A little gasp came from somewhere to Bernie's left, hastily suppressed. Bernie's eyes burned, but she remembered what Elena had said. Whatever happened she must not cry.

"And this time," Madame continued, "when you finish you *smile!*"

A feeling of relief swept over Bernie. Was that all that was wrong? She performed the *enchainement* a fourth time, straining to do it even better than before and, as her head swung round to face the mirror for the last time, she smiled until she felt like the Cheshire Cat.

"Kharashoh!" Madame called out. "Now you remember

*"Again!" Madame bit out the word that
seemed to echo round the studio.*

this. You want to dance in theatre, you *smile*!"

Falling exhausted on to the bench afterwards as she pulled on her sweater, Bernie knew it was one more thing she would never forget. Thinking again of what Elena had told her, she had a sudden hope. Madame had thought her good enough to bother about. Maybe she would have something good in the Concert Hall programme after all.

On the way back to the hostel she saw Yuri in the hall. He had arrived to escort them back to Moscow. Suddenly the world outside the school seemed real again. In three days' time they would be home.

Next day, as they got off the school bus in the station yard beneath the big clock, still faithfully keeping Moscow time, Sinéad thought how much had happened since that day in September when she had followed the others down the flight of steps which faced her now. Misha must have been amongst the boys who had loaded their baggage that day, but she had never noticed him. Now, after unloading the cases from the bus on to the trolley beside them, he stood at her side as he waited for instructions to push it up the steep incline on to the platform.

She had said goodbye to Shiori earlier in the day, before the latter left with the other Japanese girls for the airport. On arrival in Moscow, they would transfer straight to the international airport for their flight to Tokyo, instead of spending a night in the hostel like the Irish group.

"I see you in four weeks," she had said to Sinéad. "Then I bling you more special cookies. And I tell palents now I have special fliend flom Iland."

"I already wrote to Mam about you," Sinéad told her. "And when I come back I'll bring some carageen for you to try."

"What is calageen?" Shiori wanted to know.

"Irish seaweed," Sinéad told her, laughing.

"Aha! So in Iland they eat seaweed too?"

"Well, not exactly," Sinéad admitted, "but it's made from seaweed. You'll see."

"Already you back in Ireland in your head," Misha said, as she stood lost in thought.

"I was just thinking about everything that's happened since we got here," she told him. "Did you come to meet us?"

"Da, da," Misha said. "And I think: who is this small lady with the big eyes."

"I don't believe you," Sinéad laughed. "I don't believe you noticed me at all. I never noticed you."

Misha made a mock gesture of despair but, before he could speak they got the order to move up on to the platform. As he pushed the trolley up the slope with the other boys and she climbed the stairs with the girls, she didn't see him again until they had crossed the icy tracks by the sleepers on to the Up Platform. They had hardly stopped about halfway along the platform when the long train slowly chugged into the station.

"We're carriage 14!" someone yelled and there was a sudden surge up the platform as the carriages slowly pulled past them.

"Get bunks for Sinéad and me," Gráinne called unnecessarily as Bernie got first to the door and wrenched it open.

"I better go," Sinéad said.

"I bring case," Misha told her, swinging the big brown case lightly on to his shoulder.

He followed her into the compartment and dumped the case on the floor beside the little table which separated the two lower bunks. There was a sound of shouting and doors slamming.

"I think you should get off," Sinéad told Misha, "if you don't want to end up in Moscow instead of Ekaterinburg."

Misha stooped and kissed Sinéad on both cheeks before running off down the corridor. The train gave a lurch and Sinéad peered anxiously through the window to see if he had managed to get off in time but, after he had appeared on the other side of it, the train sat for several minutes while they gestured to each other, trying to talk in mime through the double pane of glass.

In the next-door compartment, Willie was gesturing in the same way to Elena. Unlike the boys, who always went to the station to help with the luggage, she had no reason to be there, but she had boarded the school bus at his side and no one had tried to stop her. On the bus he had asked her something he had thought about for the past week.

"You'll be coming to Dublin in the summer for the show in the Concert Hall, won't you?" he asked.

"I hope," Elena said.

"Well then," Willie continued, "I was thinking. The Russian students always stay in the homes of Irish students and Mum will probably be asked to take someone. She'll be expected to take a boy, but I wondered . . . well, I mean, we've a spare room and . . . well, I could ask Mum if you could stay with us if that's OK with you."

Elena gave her slow smile.

"If is OK by mother," she nodded, "I like very well."

Now she waved to him as the train finally pulled away from the platform and the cries of *Doh zveedaneeya*! Misha ran along beside Sinéad's compartment keeping pace with the train for some time until the platform ended and the train rounded a curve in the track and she could no longer see him. After they had made up their bunks and stowed away their luggage, Gráinne exchanged glances with Bernie. It was time to break the news.

"I'm going to the toilet," Bernie announced, setting off down the corridor to study the list of stations and stopping times in the case between the windows.

She wondered how long she should give Gráinne. After she had noted that, once again, the longest stopping times at stations seemed to be during the night, when they were unable to take the chance to stretch their legs, she looked out of the window for a while, but it was already too dark to see much. Surely Gráinne must have broken the news by now? Uneasily, she slid back the compartment door and glanced in.

Gráinne and Sinéad were sitting silently on either side of the compartment, staring out of the window into the darkness. Bernie, expecting tears, wondered if she had come back too soon. Could Gráinne still be trying to find the right words? Then it struck her that their positions were strangely rigid, almost like corpses. At the sound of the door sliding open, Sinéad turned to face Bernie, her face white.

"And *you* knew all about it as well!" she snarled, with an anger that took Bernie completely by surprise. "You let me go on fooling around when Mam could be dying!"

"I didn't like doing it," Bernie told her, "but Gráinne said not to tell you."

"You both make me sick!" Sinéad raged. "I don't want anything more to do with either of you. Next term I'm going to see if I can share a room with Shiori."

Strange Homecoming

"I was only doing what Mammy told me to do," Gráinne protested. "And it was Aunt Phil asked her not to tell you. She didn't want you worried when you'd a show to do."

"That was yonks ago," Sinéad snapped, "and I'm not a baby. Couldn't you have told me after the show?"

"And had you upset and worried all this time?" Gráinne asked. "By then the scare was over. Didn't you talk to Aunt Phil on the 'phone yourself?"

"Yeah, and I wondered why she sounded so odd," Sinéad cried, "and why she was out when I rang that morning. Couldn't you have said then that she was in hospital?"

"She could have told you herself if she'd wanted you to know," Bernie said gently. "It's not fair to be blaming Gráinne. She was only doing what your mother wanted and she's been worried sick. Can you not see what it's been like for her?"

Suddenly Sinéad began to cry.

"I'm sorry," she sobbed, "but I feel so awful! Not knowing when the operation is or anything. I mean, anything could be happening this minute!"

Bernie put her arm around Sinéad and drew her close.

"It's gonna be OK," she said. "I know it is. Scads of people have had that op. and been grand after. The dodgy bit was when she had the heart attack. They won't operate now till they know she'll be OK."

"I'm sorry," Sinéad said again in a muffled voice. "About what I said, I mean. You were only trying to help."

"Forget it," Bernie told her. "It was the shock."

"And when someone has a shock you're supposed to give her tea," Gráinne said briskly. "Give me your mugs and I'll get hot water from the samovar. And if I can find Yuri I'll get our sandwiches off him. I don't know about you but I'm starving."

The rest of the journey wasn't much fun. Sinéad pulled herself together and, determined to make up to the others, gave them first choice of beds in the hostel and let them decide when and where they went to do their shopping in Moscow. All the same, her white, strained face and unusual silence put a damper on the last two days and they took no part in the high jinks led by Willie and Larry.

While Gráinne bought her caviar and vodka, Sinéad went with Bernie to a street market where there were stalls selling Russian craftwork. There she found, as Misha had said she would, a penknife and a biro for Niall, and for her mother a comb in a case and a miniature balalaika, all made out of wood hand-painted in characteristic bright colours.

"She can use the comb in hospital," she said, "and if they won't let me hang the balalaika on the wall in the ward I can hang it up in her room at home for when she gets out."

"Good idea," Bernie told her, glad of the optimistic words even if Sinéad's voice seemed to shake a little.

She had herself bought penknives for her two brothers, a Russian doll for Kylie, necklaces for Eileen and Imelda and a sewing case for her mother, all of the same brightly-coloured hand-painted wooden craftwork. She had been around her mother's Moore Street stall for long enough to know how to bargain and her Russian was good enough by now to distinguish her from the tourists, who would be assumed to have dollars to burn. She had demanded reduction for quantity and had done a pretty good deal. Now they had only their fathers to worry about.

"I don't think Dad would drink vodka," Sinéad said, worried.

"I know mine wouldn't," Bernie laughed. "Pints and chasers are more his line. We'd do better in the Duty Free."

"I'd be scared we wouldn't have time or there'd be nothing I could afford," Sinéad said.

"Can't we always get them something small?" Bernie suggested, "and if we've no time in the Duty Free we'd probably get something on the plane."

In fact they had plenty of time at the airport, despite Amanda being late for the bus and all of them having to fill up forms with questions about how much money they'd had when they arrived and how much they had now.

"Nothing, is the answer to that," Bernie laughed. "I've nothing now only three English pounds and 50p and I'll need that to get Da something. It's as well Mammy's meeting me at the airport."

"I dunno if anyone's meeting me," Sinéad said shakily, but Gráinne interrupted her briskly.

"Aren't we all staying with you anyway?" she pointed out, "so you'll be coming with us."

"I suppose," Sinéad said, but she sat for most of the flight pretending to read the Russian in-flight magazine without turning the pages and only picked at the food on the little trays the hostesses handed round.

The rest of the Irish group were in high spirits, even having a singsong led by Willie, who later moved around from group to group, telling jokes, but concern for Sinéad kept Bernie and Gráinne from any wish to join in. There was a big cheer as the plane touched down on the runway but, as it taxied to a stop outside the terminal building, Bernie noticed that Sinéad's hands shook as she fumbled with the fastening of her seat belt.

Waiting for their luggage to come up on the conveyor belt, Sinéad kept glancing over towards the glass door into the arrivals lounge on the far side of the customs hall. By standing near the bank and peering at a strange angle she could just see it, but found it impossible to see the people waiting on the far side.

"Why don't you and Sinéad go on ahead," Bernie suggested. "I can wait for your cases. I oughta recognise them after falling over them every day in the room."

"Suppose they stop you going through customs?" Gráinne asked. "They're always telling you not to touch cases that don't belong to you."

"That's only in case they'd have a bomb in them," Bernie said. "Don't I know what's in yours as well as I know what's in me own?"

"All the same," Gráinne argued, "they'd make a

desperate fuss if you were caught. And there's no way Aunt Phil's gonna be out there to meet her."

"But your mother would have news of her," Bernie pointed out. "Sinéad's carrying on like a hen on a hot griddle. Couldn't *she* go on at least?"

But at that moment the conveyor belt started to roll and everyone surged forward to try to see their own cases as they swung into view.

"There's yours!" shouted Willie, as Larry's battered case tied with string around the middle came lurching around the bend in the conveyor.

"And I think the one behind it's mine," Gráinne said.

"They should all be coming soon so," Bernie said. "Weren't they all checked in together?"

"There's yours, Gráinne," Sinéad cried, "and that's mine coming now."

"OK, I'll get them," Gráinne said. "Swing your trolley round to face me."

A cheer went up in the arrivals lounge as the glass doors slid back and Michael, Richard and Amanda appeared through them at the head of the little group. Sinéad saw Aunt Nan even before Gráinne did and, leaving her trolley where it was so that everyone else had to steer their way around it, she ran over to her.

"Is Mam all right?" she cried.

"She's grand, thank God," Aunt Nan said reassuringly, as Niall appeared from behind her. "You'll be able to see for yourself tomorrow."

"I don't believe it!" Niall was saying, looking down at her as their aunt turned away to embrace her daughter. "You've got taller! Your head hardly reached my shoulder when you went away."

"Have I?" Sinéad asked. "That's good. When's Mam having her operation?"

"She had it yesterday," Niall told her. "I haven't seen her yet but they let Dad in for a while today and we can go tomorrow. He says she's going to be fine and sent you her love. They'll probably let her out in a couple of weeks, but she'll have to take it easy for a while. I do hope Aunt Nan will stay on and do the cooking."

"Of course she won't," Sinéad said. "Hasn't she been in Dublin all over the Christmas? She'll want to go home to Uncle Paddy. I'm here now."

Niall made a face.

"You mean we're going to have to put up with your cooking for the next month?" he groaned.

Sinéad laughed for the first time in two days.

"Unless you want to do it yourself," she said, "and if you don't help with the washing-up you'll get nothing."

"You've grown up as well as grown taller," Niall said in surprise, as Gráinne and her mother joined them.

As Bernie's eyes searched for her mother amongst the families lining the rails, she heard her name screamed and saw two long-legged figures in jeans hurtling towards her. Eileen beat Kylie to it by a whisker and then the three of them were hugging and screaming and laughing and crying all at once.

Robbie, Willie's younger brother, was trotting after him like a little shadow as he walked towards the exit arm-in-arm with his mother while Larry, with his mother, strolled over to his sister, still at Bernie's side though the latter was by now clasped tightly in her mother's arms.

"Are ya getting the bus into town?" Larry and Eileen's mother asked Bernie and Kylie's mother, when the greetings were finally over.

Bernie's mother nodded and the two families moved off towards the exit together.

"See ya in four week's time!" Gráinne called out to Bernie as she passed her on the way to the car park with her mother and a smiling Sinéad and Niall.

"Everything's all right, then?" Bernie asked and, as Gráinne nodded, "I thought so, when you were all gabbling away like geese."

"Sure we might as well," Gráinne laughed. "Won't we all have to turn back into swans again soon enough when we fly east again next month?"